Voices of the Valley

A Quabbin Quills Anthology

Perpetual Imagination
Boston • Northampton • New York

881 Main St #10
Fitchburg, MA 01420

info@perpetualimagination.com

Production Copyright © 2020
Quabbin Quills and Perpetual Imagination

Manufactured in The United States of America.

1 2 3 4 5 6 7 8 9 10

First Edition

ISBN: 978-1-7352576-0-0

Library of Congress Control Number in process for this title.

CONTENTS

IN MEMORY OF DENNIS KING

Quabbin Quills is honored to dedicate this anthology to the amazing Dennis King. Dennis was with us from the beginning. His enthusiasm and support helped us to grow and his love of writing and encouragement will sustain us for many years to come. He will truly be missed.

OBITUARY OF DENNIS KING

Dennis Francis King, 68, of Upton, MA passed away suddenly on December 7th 2019, surrounded by his three sons. His sons were fortunate enough to have shared one final Thanksgiving with him prior to his passing.

He was born to Marion and Walter King in Woonsocket R.I. He was the oldest of three children. Dennis attended Milford High School as part of the class of 1968. He moved to Los Angeles right after High School, right in time to experience the hippie movement at its peak. He saw The Doors live while wearing a suit and tie, but soon found his own hippie identity before seeing Hendrix and Joplin.

Dennis enlisted in the US Army in 1971, and was soon stationed in Berlin Germany as part of the Berlin Brigade. While in Berlin he was trained as a projectionist and Gama Goat driver. He was also part of the guard detail for the last remaining WWII prisoner being held at Spandau Prison, Rudolf Hess. This qualified him as a veteran of both WWII and the Vietnam war. He traveled to both sides of the Berlin Wall, an experience that forever changed him.

After his honorable discharge from the Army he achieved a degree from Sylvania Technical School for Computer Electronics and Radio/TV Electronics. He worked for 13 years at Raytheon as a Computer Systems Technician, helping to develop the Patriot Missile guidance system.

Dennis was an entrepreneur, starting several small businesses through the years, but finally discovered his love of writing. He has written several books on various topics that he self-published. He also enjoyed dancing, playing the guitar, traveling to country fairs, politics, computers and keeping junky cars on the road. Dennis was a member of the VFW, Quabbin Quills Writing Club, and a Ham Radio operator.

Dennis is survived by his brother Jamie and his wife Lindy, sister Kathy; his sons Alex, Josh, Luke, and Luke's wife Linda; and three grandchildren Shaianne, Edgar, and Victor. He also leaves behind many friends old and new. Dennis was preceded by parents Marion and Walter, and brother Gary.

BUMBLEBERRY PIE
Dennis King

Among the other pies in the country store, I saw this particular pie sitting on the table. This store was in a very rural town—where it was cheaper to buy overpriced items there than to waste gas and drive to a bigger town twenty-five miles away. They sold everything from soup to nuts—the screw kind. Many of these quaint little stores supported local farmers, selling their dairy products and even their eggs. It was a marriage of necessity.

The truth was that most of those who walked in the store only bought scratch tickets, beer, cigarettes—in that order—by mostly men. There were a few ladies who were bitten by the lottery bug, and they were seen sitting in their car—puffing a butt and scratching feverishly. It was unladylike behavior for ladies to do this in public, but when they did win, everyone heard about it. The only exception was when they hid their winnings from their husbands.

I always bought fresh honey, veggies, and corn-on-the-cob at the country store. The honey came from the man on the edge of town. The veggies and corn-on-the-cob were grown from the old couple still farming their land. The store was a good place for locals to sell their product—otherwise, no one would know where to find them.

This day was a cold, fall day. It was jackets and long-johns until next Spring. There was a nice smell in the store, so I made a cup of coffee and sat at a small table. Customers gathered there on and off during the morning—mostly to discuss the important issues of the day: bugs, rain, crops, and the wife going to the hairdresser. There were the people who would sign up to win a hunting rifle in a raffle. Hands down, their unanimous answer would be "Hell ya!" And that's including the women.

One family would bring in twenty-five fresh-baked pies first thing on Monday morning. It was first come, first serve when they arrived. The children of the family had gathered apples, pears, peaches as well as picked blueberries, strawberries, raspberries, and blackberries. They grew all these things on their property, and the money from the pie sales helped the whole family. For them, it was work if you want to eat.

It was a tradition for the women to don aprons before the pie-making. First, they peeled, soaked, and washed all the fruit. After those preparations, a decision was determined as to how many types of pies would be made. The ingredients were combined—surprisingly, no additional sugar—then pectin was added for preservation. As each pie was filled and put in the oven, some had ornate marking on the top crust. For example, an apple pie might have an apple marking.

Patiently, I sat and waited for the pie lady to arrive that early Monday morning. It was my chance to get first dibs on the selection. When she came through the door and struggled to carry the load of two dozen pies, I saw it. One pie box was labeled *Bumbleberry Pie*.

I asked her, "What the heck is a Bumbleberry Pie?" She replied that after they were done with the pies, there was always a little fruit left over. Rather than waste the extra ingredients, they were thrown into a pie crust. It seemed like it was either a waste-not want-not situation, or some bumbling idiot has estimated wrong. Regardless, I scooped up the only bumbleberry pie for this week's delivery.

Some picky eaters may turn up their nose at the potpourri—this cornucopia of treasures from Mother Nature—but not me. I ate the whole thing without sharing. This sweetness stayed on my lips and on my mind, still today.

TOO LATE

Matthew Shepardson
3rd Place Scholarship Winner

Everything was once calm now all chaotic.

My fellow brothers now lay scattered everywhere.

Some growing in pain, others gone forever.

Hoping for help to come though it may never

Ears all ringing from what sent us flying about.

Most of us didn't even see it coming.

Even if we did, what could we do?

Hope and pray for help to come.

The groaning slows as we lose the battle.

Help is too far away.

By the time they get here it will be

Too late

GREEN DARKNESS

Cecilia Januszewski
2nd Place Scholarship Winner

It's one of those nights when it feels like someone's going to get in an accident, but all you can do is cross your fingers and pray that it won't be you. A thick fog chokes the road, and rain sings as it skitters across the roof of the car. Through my half open window, a fine spray of water makes its way inside, dampening my hair. The road ahead of me is blurry and silent, and the dry scrape of the windshield wipers is soothing, even as the sound sets my teeth on edge. Squinting through the mist, I roll forward, trusting that the road's familiar curves haven't suddenly shifted. There's no one on the road with me except the raindrops, and all I can hear is the soft hiss of tires cutting through wet pavement. The wooded darkness that flanks the road is solid and imposing, and it almost seems to sneak up on you. As I speed down an empty road, I watch the dark border, aware that on the other side of the pavement civilization runs out. This is an in-between place, where the solid lines of the pavement melt into rubble, then dust. The liquid beams of my headlights barely penetrate the thick ranks of trees, and I can't shake the feeling that I'm trespassing on someone else's territory. These trees, which have already been here for a hundred years, will outlive me. When I lay decomposing they will still be strong, stretching woody fingers through the sky, and drinking in the rain.

Sometimes I dream of these trees, of their roots twisting around each other, slow-dancing in the earth beneath me. I dream of the things they wind around: rocks, animal holes, bones. Some nights I feel their roots curling around my own bones, cradling my skeleton in a tangle of ropey brown hairs and slowly crushing it. Twining between my ribs, the roots pry apart my vertebrae and lengthen my spine, contorting and twisting my silhouette. The small bones of my fingers tingle and splinter as they're slowly compressed. In these dreams I crumble, yielding to a strength far beyond my own. When I wake up, I lay gasping, partly in horror, but mostly because I miss the steady pressure of the roots between my bones. Without it, I am lonely and adrift, floating untethered through a fast-moving world. Some people are afraid of burial, and they don't like to consider their approaching demise. However, I can't help but look forward to the day when I can finally join the realm of the trees, even if that means becoming the dirt beneath them.

I used to pretend to be a tree, standing on rocks to be taller and squinting up at the sun, struggling to reach it. My hands, full of oak leaves, swayed—following the push of an imaginary wind. When I got bored of being a tree, I'd let the leaves drop one by one, watching them drift away from me and come to rest on the grass. You'd think that losing leaves would be something like getting a haircut, but when I played tree, I always felt a curious sense of loss. I imagined nurturing my own leaves, only to watch them bob away in the autumn wind and mingle in piles that looked, from a distance, like feathery brown snow. There's something rather poignant about those drifts of forgotten leaves, clinging to the trunks that bore them. It's as if they're aware of their separation, aware that no matter how high they ride the wind, they'll never manage to land back where they started. To ensure that my leaves didn't feel neglected after my game, I'd collect them and bring them up to my bedroom—planning to make sure that they were never forgotten. I'd lay them out on my desk, carefully arrange them by size, and inhale their earthy freshness. But with time, just like the trees that mothered them, I'd forget to care about them, and quietly release them back into the outdoors.

As I speed home, I feel my heart slow—relaxing into the rhythm of the rain and wind. I feel like I'm underwater, encased in a metal bubble of a car. My head fills with the loamy scent of wet leaves and I yawn, mouth wider than the moon. I'm almost home now, and the drive seems to have gone by faster than usual. On nights like this, when the only things I know for certain are the heat of the engine and the dull thump of my heartbeat, I can almost believe that I exist outside of time. If not for the glow of the dashboard clock, steadily ticking upward, I would believe it. I squint into the windshield, trying to penetrate the dark greenery ahead of me. It hums, pulling me in. As the trees that line the roadside grow ever thicker, my pulse slows,

slows,

s l o w s.

In the stillness of night rain, there is more room to breathe deeply.

I inhale and roll forward, into the green darkness.

INTO THE ROSE GARDEN

Aidan Needle
1st Place Scholarship Winner

There is a garden where these poems are

written, sheltered from the common-folk;

my own suburban cul-de-sac where

flowers forever sprout—

regardless of the season

Horticultural habitats thrive

in the winter—snow fallen from

an open mouth

//

Daily, I venture out to hang

under the dangling rubies

and write

The pathway is ingrained in my head, but

I was never brought there as a child to pick bouquets,

and each crackle of snow beneath my boots

ushers me closer to the petal laden labyrinth

that I fondly remember;

Where conversations of various flowers

are heard from afar:

the tulips gossip with the hydrangeas about the

daisies appearances

the cackling chrysanthemums can be heard in

my ears at all times;

eavesdropping on the lavenders while

I try to master their language

It takes a

while to reach the

roses; where I stand and inhale their perfumes

from a distance, they tell me to come near and sit

alongside them—take out my pen and journal

We engage in talk for a while, about

love, lust, and forgetfulness; the smaller,

younger roses have not bloomed into

conversing yet, however, the

withering ones inform me of their lives and

upbringings a little

too much

After a while

they begin to cough and grow groggy,

offering me a space to sleep for the night

Sometimes, I don't

think I am the author of my poems;

the roses simply guide my

hands

APPALACHIAN APARTMENT COMPLEX

Aidan Needle
1st Place Scholarship Winner

Decades ago I lived in a

small, rundown

tree, which harbored many

lifeforms—termites still rummage in my head:

Eating my throat,

pouring out my jowls, watering the gardens

imbedded in my

memory; how'd they crawl as night fell

to feast upon a carcass

Conversing through the hallowed walls;

disembodied calls, husband and wife—ghosts

Cries on loop like a jazz record of

beats created on the body—

saxophones of a ribcage

Every night for years they cried,

trumpets shattering glass, just

awaiting a singers lead,

He called out for months on end,

Nothing

// /

It wasn't too long until his voice drowned

in the falling water of brass,

and by that time I could no longer pay

my landlord; evicted from my

splintered suite

// /

Now, more often than not,

I lay in the near-by meadow of my arboured atrium,

staring into the velvet night, where g-d

shatters stringed constellations like tea cups

MOVING ON

Aidan Needle
1st Place Scholarship Winner

A few years back

I went to the

meadow by my old home

The trail—which led me through the mossy

overcoat of boulders until

I tumbled into a pit of pale grass—shoving me through

a new families footprints

who found inhabitancy

on the property

Two children, boy and girl

porcelain dolls of time—rummaging in my

forgotten foliage; throwing handfuls of

orange, red, and brown up into the lithosphere

//

Interludes of a memory:

Laying down on the daisey filled

plain to inhale the scents of mint and

thyme that grew in the

gardens that circled my home—

Cyphining tea from spiles

stabbed through the body of a rotted maple stump;

an excavated bladder

//

That house, that meadow,

my old lover, who lived with me

and their aquamarine dreams

of being the next best american

author; the times

I lay in baths of dandelion milk,

dreaming of somewhere else—on my own

//

They sleep in prose,

and I leave, the last of the ink running from a pen

But what about these children, across the forest boundaries,

who dream of marzipan skies?

I turned

away from them,

Looked back, and saw

Nothing.

DISPATCH FOR THE EARTH

Eileen Kennedy

I am writing to you, earth, ground, sod
from a place where farmers, artists, liberals,
conservatives, students, carpenters, dreamers live.
This is the platform, the space
that makes the base
for what we call home.

It's about dairy cows twitching black gnats,
strawberry preserves spreading on rye bread,
book stores lodging in fly-coated horse fields,
farm trucks fuming at $5 car washes,
laptops padding Route 9 strip malls,
vegetable stands counting tin can cash.

This dispatch is for the dirt
that farmers grow vegetables in.
The tree roots, pinecones, rocks that we walk on.
I praise every day it happens,
the astonishing in the common
in my little town.

Published in Compass Roads: A Dispatch from Paradise/Poems about the Pioneer Valley, edited by Jane Yolen and the Straw Dogs Writers Guild, Levellers Press 2018 and Poems from the Wellspring, Poetic License 2019.

ASHFIELD
Eileen Kennedy

Twilight rain on lake

Silence of absent children

Cars driving nowhere

Published in Rockhurst Review in 2006.

THE BOTTOM OF THE FOOD CHAIN

Diane Kane

"You ain't never goin' make it," Walter told me on my first day of training at the Athol Post Office. Walter was a crusty old bugger. He was a rural mail carrier. They're a special breed—combination pack mule and stallion.

When I was hired as Walter's substitute, I was told that I would work his mail route every Saturday and any day that Walter wanted off. I wasn't told that Walter had gone through thirty-two subs in twenty years. There was no doubt about the number because Walter had a notch cut into his mail case for each one of them.

The first day Walter took me out to train on his mail route, he drove, and I put the mail in the mailboxes. I worked tirelessly while Walter chewed on his tobacco and told stories.

"Twenty years ago, when I started carrying mail, I used to carry a gun under my seat," He said. "Not to shoot the customers," he assured me. "Though, sometimes I'd like to. There's all kinds of varmints out here in the sticks, ya know."

"No," I stammered. "What kind of varmints?"

"Well, girly, there's b'ar, wolves, and moose. Make no mistake, them there moose can be as nasty as all get out when they got young 'uns. They don't scare me none, I'm a stubborn old Yankee," he said with pride.

One particular customer that day had a package that looked a little too big to fit in the mailbox. When I pointed this out to Walter, he wiped the chewing tobacco spit from his chin and grabbed the package out of my hand. I watched as he put it between himself and the steering wheel and pushed. I heard a loud crack that I imagined was more than the cardboard box changing shape.

"There," he said. "Now stuff it in the mailbox like I told you. Never forget, girly, you're at the bottom of the postal food chain.

***

The next day I attended more training at the postal facility in Amherst, Massachusetts. As I sat among a dozen other newly hired rural carrier substitutes at the bottom of the food chain, I pondered my future with the Postal Service.

That was when the president of the Rural Carriers Union paid a visit to the class. He asked us all our names and what post office we would be working.

"Oh," he said to me. "We got a call about you."

"Me?" I said with a sinking feeling.

"Yes. A Mrs. Miller came into the Athol Post Office yesterday carrying her mailbox under her arm. She put it on the counter and told the mail clerk to see if he could get the package out. It took him some time, and when he did—well—did you bend that book in half?"

"No! Walter did."

"Well, that's what we thought, but Walter said you did it."

I brooded in class all day. When it was over, I raced back to the Athol Post office. I arrived just as Walter was getting back from his route.

"Why did you tell them I bent that book?" I said as I pounded his arm with my fist.

Just then, the postmaster saw me and called me into his office.

On his desk sat a mangled cardboard box. Sitting sadly on top of the box was a hardcover Time/Life book with large creases the entire length of the front and back covers.

"Did you bend that book in half?" the postmaster asked.

"No, sir, I did not."

"That's what I thought ... WALTER!"

I had a big smirk on my face as I walked out of the office and as Walter was walking in.

About twenty minutes later, Walter came out carrying the book with two broken covers.

"I had to pay for the book," he said. "I think you should pay half."

"I don't think so, Walter, and I can be just as stubborn as you are."

"Well," he said. "I guess I'll go home and read my book."

"I think she's goin' make it after all," I heard him mumble as he walked away.

I had a funny feeling that we both learned a lesson that day.

It was shortly after that he stopped calling me girly. Instead, I would hear him tell people, "That's my girl," and I could hear the pride in his gravelly voice.

Against all odds, Walter and I became the best of friends. He taught me how to be tough, and I taught him that he didn't always have to be.

Walter retired from the post office, and two years later, he passed away.

I moved up the postal food chain. Now, I have my own route. Some days when I'm at a mailbox with a package that's just a little too big to fit in the box, I smile and think of Walter. As I do the right thing and walk the package to the door, I can hear Walter's voice saying, "That's my girl." I can't help but get a little misty-eyed—because that's what crusty old buggers will do to you sometime.

NOT A PLACE OF LOSS

Sharon Harmon

Take me to an azure sky,

to not a place of loss.

But to a place of what can be

to an uplifting hope of things

where we can soar on feathered wings.

Where mountains meet skyline,

and there are pictures in the roots of old oak trees.

Where leaf patterns have mysteries to whisper.

Where imprints of ferns etched into rock

tell the solidity of frailness.

A place where cloth puffs of clouds

scud together in picture images

and vibrant trees meet tangled shore.

Where unexpected wild flowers

speak of life's surprises and

possibility and more.

A liquid place of beauty to

quench our souls thirst

where raindrops may strike a

pond, resonating in ripples of the truth.

Echoes off the mountains edge

repeat its stone messages over and over.

We are good.

We are here.

We are now.

Let us have heartfelt conversations in the

deep woods of our desire,

not a place of loss.

SNOWY WOODS

Diana Lynne Norman

Exquisite snowflakes drift,

my wide eyes

spot them all around.

My bedtime has come and gone.

How astonishingly moon and snow link,

creating this magical glitter-land.

Snow is a soft rabbit muff

allowing quiet to rule the woods

beneath the starlight.

Our boots, the only tracks

on this lonely lane

carry us soundlessly deeper

into the tree branches

heavy with layers of white.

Beneath my woolen scarf

my cheeks tingle

with the sting of winter's crisp exhalation.

Tiny puffs of my warm breath drift

to merge with the night's magic.

His big leather work glove

engulfs my scratchy blue mitten

keeping me warm

keeping me safe.

Gently he tugs my arm.

I look up to Daddy's face.

It's tilted toward the stars.

He points.

I see it too:

a falling star!

I squeeze my eyes tight

make my special wish

in the midst of that magical night.

Dream imagined.

I gaze into Daddy's face again.

His twinkling blue eyes dance as they meet mine.

He removes his gloves and signs,

"What did you wish for?"

I shake my head:

Everyone knows your wish won't come true, if you tell.

THE LEMON RIND

Sonya Shaw

Ah, the lemon rind.

How sweetly your bitterness

Rests densely on my pallet.

I remember the taste

that harshly awakened me from my bliss.

I remember begging not to take you,

I wished it wasn't so.

I thought you'd break me,

For I was unaware of my own strength.

I had tucked you away for a while.

Left you to dry and allow

Your color to fade,

Your pulp to shrivel

And skin to whither.

But here you are

Shouting for my attention.

Brighter, more lively

And just as potent as you were

The day I placed you in that box.

Labeled, stacked and stored

On the shelf with the other moments

That tried to take away my sweetness.

You may think your pungency is strong

And your skin is thick,

But you have witnessed just a mere grain of my sugar,

And I have learned to carry more.

I had once taken you with resistant hands

And apprehensive arms.

I objected,

I fought

and attempted to control you.

I was not fooled by your bright yellow skin.

I was not teased by the juice

that fled from your flesh

when you were cut,

squeezed and sent to the bottom of the pitcher.

Sure, my lips puckered.

My eyes watered.

But I was not scathed.

I added the water

And gathered spoon after spoon of sugar.

I left you no option but to spin and stir,

Twist and turn.

Forcing you to absorb

every ounce of your bitterness

into cups of sweet lemonade.

You challenged my determination,

And questioned my strength

But I prevailed.

I drank every—single—drop.

You quenched my thirst,

And I was finally satisfied.

But here in front of me,

Lie once again the lemon rinds.

How bold of you to show up after all this time.

You dare to make me bitter again?

Little do you know my dear,

My pockets are full of honey

And damn is it sweet.

A REGALSTONE THANKSGIVING
Kathy Chencharik

"Another cup, John?" Kitty picked up the pot of coffee and brought it over to the kitchen table.

"Sure." Constable John St. John put down the Regalstone Newsletter he'd been reading and smiled at his wife.

Kitty glanced down at the newsletter and pointed to an article. "Next week is Thanksgiving," she said, pouring coffee. "The way I see it, we have two choices. One, we could invite Esther Forbes here for Thanksgiving dinner, or B, we could volunteer to help out at the senior center's Thanksgiving meal."

"I'd have to choose B. Don't you remember what happened last year when we invited Esther over on Christmas Eve? We asked her if she wanted a glass of wine. She not only polished off the bottle, she passed out on the couch and spent the night."

Kitty chuckled at the memory. "Then, she woke up in the middle of the night, saw you heading for the bathroom in your red union suit, and thought you were Santa Claus." Her chuckle turned to laughter. She laughed so hard, tears rolled down her cheeks. "I still have a picture of her sitting on your lap."

"Keep it up and I'm going to get rid of that camera of yours."

"Oh, no you won't. Don't forget it came in handy before."

"How could I forget?" John finished his coffee and headed for the door. "Sign us up to volunteer. Come on, Hoover, time to protect and serve. The weather is unseasonably warm and we can take Old Blue."

The little white Bichon got up from his doggie bed next to the kitchen table. He stretched, wagged his tail, and followed John outside. John lifted Hoover up and placed him into the milk crate attached to the back fender of his blue bicycle.

On Thanksgiving morning, John and Kitty drove their green Ford F-150 truck to the town hall on Regalstone Common. John nodded toward Officer Dale Roland, dressed in uniform, who was going to give a talk after the meal about all the scams seniors face this time of year.

Because of the holiday, The Bushwhacker, the only country store in town, was closed. Pat Bushwhacker, owner of the store, and Town Clerk Betty "Boom Boom" Reed were in the kitchen peeling potatoes.

"I see you two got KP duty," Kitty said with a smile. "What would you like me to do?"

"Ask them." Pat pointed behind her. "The Ladies Benevolent Society runs this show. We just do what they say."

Kitty turned. Four members of the LBS were putting turkeys into the ovens. She walked over to Mo Blacklist. "What would you like John and I to do, Mo?"

"You could set up the tables," she said, wiping sweat off her brow. "Thanks for helping."

"Right back at ya. You women do so much for this town." Kitty left the kitchen in search of John.

When John and Kitty had finished setting up tables, they heard a commotion coming from outside the dining area. They peered through the open door. Esther Forbes was carrying a large pocketbook with one hand while brandishing her cane with the other. She pushed her way through the crowd of elderly people.

"Esther, watch the cane," John admonished. "You almost took the toupee off of Earl."

"Thanks, Constable. I'm glad I came too. But squirrel? I know we have an abundance of them in town, but I was really hoping for turkey."

John groaned, shook his head, and wondered if he made a mistake with his choice. He watched Mrs. Kettle settle Earl's toupee back in place. Arm in arm, John and Kitty entered the dining area—avoiding Esther as they took a seat at one of the tables.

"Why is everyone here so early?" John asked as the room filled up with the elderly.

"Bingo!" shouted Esther. She took a seat and placed her large pocketbook on a chair beside her.

"You heard me that time?" John asked.

"What? No. I'm warming up to play bingo."

Mo Blacklist heard the ruckus and came to Constable John's aid.

"Esther," she said loudly, "I know we usually play bingo, but not today. Today is Thanksgiving, and everything's all set up for dinner. After we eat, Officer Dale wants to speak to everyone about scams."

"Hams?" Esther asked, making a face. "First it's squirrel. Now it's hams? What happened to turkey?"

Mo couldn't help but laugh. She bent down and shouted into Esther's ear, "We are having turkey, Esther."

"Thank goodness. For a minute I thought I was going to have to leave."

"Please take it back, Mo," John whispered in her ear. "Tell her we are having squirrel."

ADDISON FRENCH BURNISHES HER SEARCH FOR IDENTITY
Sally Sennott

"In France, they have a saying that goes something like this: No matter where you land, you need to be able to flower."

~*Anonymous*

In the beginning theirs was a needy love. Both Addie and Nelson were divorced and caring for kids. By blending their families, they created a grouping with both a mother and a father.

Addison and Nelson pretended to marry. There was a ceremony, and they went through the motions. Their vows were jointly written and sincere. There was no accompanying paperwork. The children were in their teens, and there was college tuition to consider. Student loans would be more favorable if there were a single parent earning income, and so, it was decided: diamond ring and wedding band? Yes. But a certificate of marriage? Nself-centeredo.

Pushing 40 and still beautiful, Addison wore a simple dress and lace mantilla on that hot June day on Long Island. Nelson was dressed in a navy-blue suit and red tie with a matching red carnation boutonniere. He was short and a bit on the chubby side, but together they made a dashing couple. Actually, this was important because they both used to turn heads when entering a venue. Nelson was a salesman and knew how to work a room. Addison's upturned nose, Elizabeth Taylor brows, and matching eyes set her apart. Even at her age, her Irish skin was still taut. And Nelson loved her for all these traits.

Nelson sold jeans for a living, and the Gloria Vanderbilt style was popular back in 1980 when their love was new. Now, nearly 40 years later, needy love had not morphed into giving love. Addie had put on weight and was critical of Nelson's habit of falling asleep in his chair in the early evening. He, in turn, put Addison under pressure to continue to look good and be the life of the party. The couple still liked to make an entrance at events. Dressed up, they still were an eye-turning twosome.

Addie would diet for the family wedding pictures, losing 25 pounds only to gain it back. Appearances counted for everything. They lived on Addison's generous nursing director's pension and saved her small Social Security check for Christmas presents for their 13 grandchildren. Nelson had invested his inheritance in the stock market and had Social Security for routine expenses. However, the couple liked to live large and they strained to make ends meet. Addison continually toyed with the question: "What do I want?" Nelson seemed obliged to give into her fiscal whims. Financial red flags were ignored and consequences went unweighted. It was a superficial lifestyle, and underneath the foundation was giving way. Their common law marriage was in trouble.

Did they fight? Not so much. But contempt is deadly and Nelson's feeling of self-worth suffered from bouts of recurring depression. As for Addie, although she knew she lived a privileged lifestyle, the cost of always doing what others expected of her was taking its toll. Beauty fades, and children and grandchildren move away and establish independent lives. Her purpose in life, directing the family's activities, was coming to a close. She had peaked early and like an elite athlete, had to cope with finding other fulfilling activities. She was an empty nester and had no deep feelings for her husband, whom she had no interest in caring for in old age. Death and dying were not in her repertoire although she would turn seventy-seven in the fall. Shallow and self-centered, her moral isolation and loneliness caused her terrible suffering.

Addison had not been given the gift of unconditional love as a child. She was Daddy's little girl. Yet Helena, her Mother, was ever critical and had favored her younger brother. Addison had to earn her Mother's love through accomplishments. In the early years, she excelled at ballet that spilled over into jitterbugging at high school dances. She was a social butterfly and always had partners to jive with. She moved in the fast lane and branched out to surrounding towns.

At 19, Addison found herself pregnant. She had been sleeping around at college and at home on vacations. She chose as her first husband her true love, who as it turned out was not the father of her baby. The marriage was annulled, and she rushed off to Long Island and married the baby's biological father.

Two babies later, she discovered her second husband was cheating on her. Addie had gone to college to find a husband and had no real academic interests. Yet, she had to find a vocation. She now had a reason to apply herself, so went back to college and earned a Masters in Nursing Management. She sought work, and found employment as head nurse at a large psychiatric hospital.

At this point, stomach problems and panic attacks began to plague her. For example, she was afraid to ride in the elevator, and Addison's office was on the third floor. She took to coming into work two hours early, so she could be escorted in by the kindly "man of color" who operated the cage through its hoisting machinery which conveyed her to the third level. It seemed as though his soothing presence made the assent plausible.

Addison had the need to be taken care of. She had been born to this role that was further defined by the societal norms of the fifties while she was growing up. During her formative years, middle class women did not work, and in her daydreams, she wanted to be married and living in a nice house with adorable children.

Addison's childhood bedroom was filled with dolls. The room had once been a kitchen, and the high cabinets behind her double bed were decorated with expensive dolls on display. China head dolls and standing dolls dressed in the finery of foreign countries graced the open shelves. She was raised to find a husband who could support her in the style in which she had grown up. The corner house was in the center of town and her mother hobnobbed with the rich neighbors. Surely this lifestyle, based on male support, would be hers in adulthood.

Jeffrey, Addison's father, had a midlife crisis though, and bought a Thunderbird. His pharmacist business wasn't prospering, and they had to move out of the corner house. Addison went off to college in Florida but after one year transferred to a small school in Ithaca, New York. She grew up to be a doll, a pretty but empty-headed young woman. Cheerleading was her vocation, and she captained the squad.

As a result of Addie's life experiences up to age 20 or 21, she developed a lifelong fear of abandonment. Mental happiness eluded her and she struggled to find calm in her existence. After retirement, traveling and one activity after another filled her days. Changing the status quo did not change the inner turmoil. But Addison could not stand the doldrums and tedium of the quotidien either. Always a cheerleader, she had to be meeting and greeting new people and presenting herself as a charming individual. Addison could put on a show, yes, like a movie star puts on a show; but donning sunglasses at the restaurant table is laughable at age 76. Even in the evening light, the wrinkles are there. Chronically bored and dissatisfied with her existence, she could never find peace.

Addison's emotional growth was stunted. She could not answer the big question: "What is life asking of me?" for she did not know what she wanted. Fear was always lurking in the background. She was the proverbial spoiled, insecure woman.

It's no wonder that as Nelson aged, he was beset with depression. He was saddled to a wife incapable of growing up. Her wants and expectations were endless. He was cast in the role of rescuer, and Addie was the victim. They never switched roles in 40 years of married life.

Take her funeral plans for instance. Addison simply skipped over the process of dying and demanded a Marilyn Monroe funeral. Her fantasy was limousines and a flower bedecked casket with hundreds paying homage—after being flown from Florida to Long Island where her children and grandchildren still resided. Money was no object in her dreams. A crowd in mourning for her absence, tears and banks of flowers were necessary. Yet, she could not temper her demands in the here and now to pay for this lavish funeral. Even when told by financial advisors she must cut back on her lifestyle, a showy funeral somehow became more of a necessity. She refused to go to seminars that explained the advantages of cremation. Being scattered to the winds offered no appeal. A big, massive, and expensive headstone *did* appeal.

"There is no loneliness so lonely as the loneliness you feel when you are lying there loveless in bed with another."

~David Brook

Addison knew she was no longer in love with Nelson, but was powerless to act. After all, she was deathly afraid of being alone with herself. Addison yearned for emotional intensity and Nelson being her fountain of love was an impossible job—as hard as Sisyphus rolling the stone up the mountainside. Addie stayed with Nelson because he loved her so intensely. She could not bear to be loved in a mediocre manner. Being alone was the only thing worse than bearing her actual life. She felt misunderstood, but it was her own fault. Even Addison herself could not face the cracks in the foundation of her personality.

As her marriage broke down, Addison suffered. Even her therapist had been unsuccessful in abetting Addie to reach her inner self. Addison would repeat her mantra out loud: "I live in Naples, Florida, in a lovely place, in a beautiful house with new furniture and a lovely pool; with casual friends with whom to bowl and play mahjong and bocce and go out to dinner. I have a husband, children and grandchildren. I have a lovely life. Why can't I find peace?"

The saying 'No Pain, No Gain' did not speak to her. Childlike, she had peaked in late adolescence and could not see beyond the tragedy of losing her true love. Yet, her bargain with the devil was becoming harder and harder to bear. The dance recitals were so very long and the sporting events she had been cheering at for 55 years were not quite so exciting. These activities with her grandchildren were no longer enough. All she truly had was her fading looks, her children and grandchildren, an unfulfilling marriage, and a Facebook following of employees dating back ten years to when she was the Director of Nursing at Creedmoor, the second largest psychiatric hospital in the state of New York.

Even her best friend offended her sensibilities by the constant comparison of her devotion to her husband. Elise would get in the shower with her disabled husband. This prospect drove Addison to distraction. She would never face a future of decline no matter how intensely Nelson loved her. On the other hand, she wanted people to think her capable of showing that kind of love, but a needy love rarely morphs into giving love, and theirs was no exception.

"What sort of person have I become?" Addison asked herself occasionally. She did not know that you learn through suffering, not happiness. She had been wounded several times— knee operations, a broken arm—but never had she confronted real illness and deprivation. Eyelid surgery? Yes. A tooth implant? Of course. But it was never chemo, radiation, and the threat of death. Isolated from hardship by her trips to the shopping mall and trendy restaurants, as well as her trophy trips to the national parks, she had always led a cushy life buffered from falls. The greatest pain Addison ever felt was in her wallet, and with five kids, there was always one who required rescue.

Most recently, it was her stepson, Jacob, the black sheep of the flock. While hosting his family at Verona Walk, in between swimming in the pool and ample meals, Jacob cornered Nelson and convinced his father to lend him 10K, ostensibly to make a down payment on a rent-to-own property. Supposedly, it was the landlord who required this show of good faith, but no papers have been signed and Jacob was a mortgage broker. Meanwhile, this scenario seemed fake and highly suspicious to Addison. Moreover, she had been asked to keep the transaction a secret from Jacob's wife. And to add insult to injury, Nelson proposed using the money in Addison's credit card account which offered free interest for one year.

In frustration, Addison sent an email to her longtime high school friends: *I can't stand this anymore! I am not the same person as I appear on the outside.* With her good credit in jeopardy and the strain too much to bear, Addison was aroused to a new point of risk taking—ready to shed the ego and take off the mask so her new self could emerge.

And so, Addison entered into a new modus operandi: indifference. Indifference toward Nelson falling asleep in the recliner. Indifference toward him reminding her that it is time for her to attack her chin fuzz. Indifference to the needs of his adult son. The financial plot was at long last an affliction she could understand. The health of her marriage was at stake. Addison's high school friends were already divorced or widowed and unsaddled by a husband. She was standing on new ground and didn't know what to make of it. Would she be able to fight off contempt for Nelson? Everyone knows that a couple can fight, but when contempt creeps into a relationship, the end is near.

"I want to be the person I am when I'm alone with my thoughts while reading a book," Addison would fantasize. *"It is my life. The turning point has come."* Now there will be a cutting remark when raising the Riesling glass, and it will be at Nelson's expense. But will change go so far as to

take over the checkbook? Only time would tell. This was a new beginning; a seizing of initiative. *"Let the ego die,"* Addie thought. *"Forget trying to impress others. I will do it for myself and myself alone."*

Change is a three-step process: from suffering to wisdom to service. Addison would not take all three steps. She seriously considered picking herself up and going out into the world—leaving Nelson and getting an apartment on her own—a different physical space away from her beloved house in Naples. Perhaps she *would* pursue a new way of being after all. She would be strong and test her intuition—be quiet and still. Learn self-love. Leave behind all the people-pleasing habits that had become interwoven into her personality and family life.

"Please yourself for a change. Get to know the emerging you. Let your illusions die," she counseled herself. Suffering this financial affront had upset the normal pattern of life. Forced to face that she was not who she thought she was, she reminded herself that suffering called for a mature response, not a party. It was the beginning of an independent life.

"You are not an appendage. You are complete in yourself," Addison mused.

Her self-sacrifice was no longer making sense to her. She had lost a sense of purpose in her life, and she would have to find it again. She now had the wisdom, but what of the service? No longer the victim of a loveless marriage, she now had hope. The time for change had come. Caring for herself through pampering had been easy, but living independently, devoid of her creature comforts, would be the hardest service work she had ever imagined.

The only thing that scared her was possibly breaking a nail … and she could live with that.

SEARCHING FOR HERMES

Phyllis Cochran

"Mom, look at Hermes," my son called.

I walked into the hallway. The neighborhood children lined up to watch Michael's hamster crawl up the flight of stairs. When Hermes reached the top, the children squealed with joy.

Ten-year-old Michael had bought his pet with his birthday money and spent days exercising him until his pet crawled up all sixteen stairs. Hermes became the center of attention. He amused everyone.

Kristen, Michael's sister, sat by Hermes' cage. She saw her brother carefully pick the little fellow up and let him eat out of his hands. She saw him tumble around in his play-wheel.

One afternoon, Michael asked his sister, "Will you take Hermes into the bathroom and let him walk around while I'm gone? Make sure you close the door so he won't get away."

Kristen's eyes sparkled. Now, she could play with Hermes by herself. She held him in her hands just like Michael had done. She stroked his head. Gently, she set him down and watched him scamper across the floor.

After a few minutes, Kristen shouted. "Mom! Mom! Hermes is gone. He squeezed through that little opening," she said, pointing toward the water pipe under the bathroom cabinet.

The search for Hermes began. Michael arrived home and learned his hamster was missing. He began calling out, "Hermes! Hermes!"

Michael raced up to the attic with Kristen close behind. They called his name and listened for a sound. They tramped down two flights of stairs to the cellar, all the while chanting his name. Late into the night, the whole family listened for sounds inside the bathroom cabinet.

Michael and Kristen darted from room to room calling, "C'mon Hermes! C'mon Bug-a-boo!" Before going to bed, they recorded their calls and let it play in a loop in the bathroom cabinet.

The next morning, I phoned the tenants living in our downstairs apartments. "Michael's hamster is missing. If you hear any sounds in the ceiling or in the walls, please let us know," I said.

Everyone living in the house grew quiet. Days passed with everyone in the house pinning their ears against the walls and listening for Hermes.

One day Eleanor, the woman living on the first floor, thought she heard a faint scraping sound overhead. When my husband Phil arrived home from work, he grabbed some tools and began prying up floorboards inside a closet on the second floor. Still, no Hermes. Phil even squeezed into a tight area in an unfinished room and crawled on his stomach with a flashlight to peer down between partitions. He risked getting stuck. He'd do anything for his children.

"I can't stand it. I keep thinking about Hermes starving or dying of thirst," Michael said, his voice quivering. "It's been a week."

"Maybe we should pray," I said.

We stood in a circle and held hands. I had no idea how to pray.

"Please God," I began, "watch over Hermes. Keep his stomach full when it's empty even when he has no food or water."

On the eleventh day in the evening, Joanne, another tenant, called saying, "I hear a scratching noise in my bathroom. Maybe it's Hermes."

Phil leaped up from the table where he had been sipping coffee with our friends, Jim and Jean. He grabbed a cutting tool and headed for the stairs.

"You aren't really going to cut through the ceramic tile in the bathroom, are you?" Jim asked, following close behind.

"Guess I'll have to," Phil said. "I have to try. The sound might be Michael's hamster."

Phil cut the tiles to make an opening in the bathroom wall. Hermes, weak and unable to move, lay scrunched up in a corner. His back legs curled under him. The tiny little fellow could not stand or feed himself.

"I knew Hermes would let us know if he was alive," Michael yelled, reaching out to cushion Hermes in his hands.

At bedtime, I held hands with Michael and Kristen and we prayed. "Thank you, God, for helping us find Hermes and for taking care of him."

Michael began nursing his hamster back to health by feeding him droplets of water. Slowly, he began to nibble food. Before long, Hermes learned to sit, stand, and hold nuggets between his paws. Again, he scurried through the tubular apparatus attached to his cage.

One afternoon, I overheard voices coming from behind the front door. Children were squealing. I peeked around the corner to see Hermes crawling up the stairs. He slipped back then crept forward. When he reached the top, the neighborhood children cheered louder than ever.

I turned back toward the kitchen and whispered, "Thank you, God, for Michael and Kristen's faith."

HEMLOCK HOSPICE

Karen Traub

As they lose their needles and then their life

I watch the giants fall

I think of every person I have known and loved who has died

And I remember to live

New life will sprout from this decay

There will be more light in the forest

More sun in the winter

And a view of the dawn each new day

GUITAR DEMISE
Jennifer Delozier

I had a dream.

Jimi Hendrix at the Brass Cat.

Patrons spilling

out into the street.

Darkness. Rainy sky

pouring down upon us like gloom.

Lightning crashing;

sending messages to the earth.

His guitar

beaten, demolished.

Fans screaming, berserk.

Pieces flying everywhere;

music pulsating with

loud and harmful sounds.

In guitar heaven it now rests;

strings floating on billowy clouds.

MUSIC IS A SAVAGE BEAST

Steven Michaels

Music is a savage beast

Forget about the taming

A Beast is drawn to dulcet tones

because they speak the same language

Baroque pieces of long ago

are but terriers on a leash

Classically trained

Opera Housebroken

Learnéd men still like

the company they keep

Twas Jazz which reminded us

what many had forgotten

that the howling

and the thumping

were but natural progressions

listen to the Armstrongs

improvise a tune

commanding mongrel notes

to speak

lessons learned

at disobedience school

The kennel called Time Signature

busted up by rock and roll

The electrifying current

let loose the dogs of war

Wild Notes

High Pitched Wails

Say nothing of the golden scales

climbing up stairways to Heaven and

cruising down highways to Hell

Eagles over Hotels in California

Def Leopards and White Snakes everywhere

Karma Chameleons hiding behind

Boy Georges of the Jungle

crooning to those Monkees and Hepcats

Minotaur Waltzes

Octave-pusses

Giraffe-Clefs

Allegro-gators

Fortissi-mouse

Stork-catta

Hummingbirds

a Whole Carnival of Animals

wedged into pastures

we call measures

tamed by instruments

or dominant vocals

Melody is but a chain

holding back the Beast

sprung from the mind and breast

of the most savage creature of all

THE JOURNEY OF THE ORANGE BLOCK

Phyllis Cochran

Three containers had caught my eye when I stored away winter clothes in the attic. Purposefully, they were tucked away where they would be protected—untouched by others. Beneath plastic lids, lay dolls, a jewelry box, a ballerina outfit, hundreds of cards, and other special possessions once belonging to our daughter, Susan.

She had fallen seriously ill and died from a brain tumor shortly before her ninth birthday. Several times I attempted to sort out the contents but ended up mourning for what could never be. That particular day I felt strong, ready for the task. I had reclined on the top attic stair, immersed in yesterdays' past.

While smoothing out Raggedy Ann's apron, I whispered, "It was you, Raggedy, who rode into surgery cuddled in Susan's arms when we were forbidden."

I moved the disks in the Booby Trap game. I could almost hear Susan giggling in bed while entertaining her chums. His plaything had given her joy when her vision dimmed and only one hand remained usable. It and the other tangible belongings left behind brought comfort to me over the years. They had become my treasures.

When I reached into one box, I pulled out a fistful of Susan's second-grade classmates' hand-drawn cards. I often thought of these as my 'box of love'. Lopsided lettering scrawled comforting words across art paper adorned with pictures. Loving messages leaped off the paper and grabbed me—causing a lump to form in my throat. Although I knew these were meant for my formerly ill daughter, I had a great deal of trouble parting with them. I decided to select only a few for safekeeping and dispose of the remainder.

I carried the box downstairs to the living room. Just as I began sorting through the cards, my five-year-old granddaughter, Jessica, threw open the door. Lost in my private world, I had forgotten I was taking care of her after kindergarten.

"What are you doing, Granny?" She asked, leaning over my arm.

"I'm sorting your Aunt Susan's cards," I said. "You can help. I'll pass you the ones for the trash."

"Look at the yellow daisy. You can't throw this one away. It's too pretty," she insisted after I slipped the first in her direction.

"Set some aside for yourself," I said, retrieving another bag.

A few hundred cards later, Jess' sack was overflowing. The one for disposal remained empty. Suddenly, Jess latched onto an orange block buried beneath the pile of cards. It bore the words SUSAN'S BLOCK in black lettering.

"Can I keep this?" Her brown eyes sparkled as she admired the bits of colorful fabric and buttons glued in a collage-like manner.

"Take this," I said, handing her a purple-painted, oddly shaped wooden craft.

"No, I want the orange one," she insisted, tugging on the object.

"But Jessica, orange was Susan's favorite color, and her name is on it," I said, playing tug of war with the chunky creation. "What would you want it for?" I asked.

"I'll take it to show and tell. Then I'll put it on my desk."

I loved my grandchildren and would give them almost anything. But this? This was Susan's last creation. I set the block aside. Jess looked down in disbelief as she turned her attention back to the cards.

In silence, I struggled. Susan no longer needed hidden attic treasures. Letting go of this craft could never bring Susan back. I would never forget her. Already, I was storing up special memories with our grandchildren. The future and renewed happiness stood before me. I released the chunky wooden object into my granddaughter's hands. The next day, Jessica showed Susan's block to her kindergarten class and told how it had been created.

Throughout elementary school and high school, Susan's block sat on Jessica's desk in her bedroom. She stored it in a safe place when she left for college.

Years passed. By now, I had forgotten about the orange block. Jess and her husband, Eric, were now raising three children. My life had become filled with joy. I was making special memories with my great-grandchildren. While visiting their home one day, five-year-old Evelyn asked me to come with her to her room so we could do a fun project together. I leaned back on her bed scanning the room. There, sitting on Evelyn's bureau, set the orange block. SUSAN'S BLOCK, I read. I smiled, remembering the day I had released this object into Jessica's hands at the same age.

Time had passed—sad moments spent in the valleys of life, joyful moments on the mountain tops. Today, I reminisce over the journey of the orange block.

Once again it sets in the light—no longer stored in a tub in the attic.

A version of this story was previously published in Chicken Soup for the Soul – Devotional Stories for Tough Times in 2011

REMEMBER
Christina Sutcliffe

Look across the surface

> (which mirrors heaven

> with minimal earthly interference)

As the loon flies

> (wingtips inches from a reflection

> supplementing reality)

And see a *virgin* landscape

> (hillocks of oak, hemlock and

> miles of water lapping at asphalt shores).

Unseen, the valley

> (sloping down from roads

> gone ghostly to their depths)

Whispers names

> (Dana, Enfield,

> Greenwich, Prescott)

Lost to *progress*

> (hundreds of millions thirsting

> bathing in this lake of memories).

QUABBIN'S CHILD

Marie LeClaire

Saturday morning was overcast as Michelle wriggled into her Spandex shorts and tied on neon green running shoes. She checked the weather out the kitchen window before making her final decision. Low clouds, heavy with moisture, were promising rain before the day's end, but it looked like the morning would be dry.

During the week, she stuck to a routine that started and ended at the back door. On the weekends, she allowed herself a little extra time to run through the nature preserve. It was the best way she knew to leave the work week behind and start the weekend with a clean slate. Today's route was a ten-mile loop through Quabbin Reservoir, starting at Gate 40.

As she drove to the reservoir entrance, the cloud ceiling lowered itself, and a light fog hovered just above the power lines. As long as it wasn't full-on raining when she got to the entrance, she told herself, the run was a go.

She'd run all of the old roads of Quabbin over the past few years, but she liked this particular route the best. It had long gradual inclines and a water view. More than that, it gave her a sense of what had come before—before Boston flooded four towns to create one of the largest public water supplies on the planet. She tried not to think of it that way, but running past the old cellar holes and sidewalks-to-nowhere touched her heart. Her mind would wander, thinking about the nearly three thousand lives, as well as family farms and businesses, that once thrived here. She tried to imagine what it must have looked like.

In the end, the resulting watershed had become a wildlife refuge and a destination for hikers, bikers, and boaters. It currently boasted nine pairs of nesting bald eagles. As beautiful as it is, its history held a shadow over her enjoyment of it, which felt like a guilty pleasure.

By the time she parked the car, the cloud ceiling had settled to the ground, and fog hovered over the moist roadways. She considered the limited visibility conditions, then decided she'd run this route often enough to navigate it without a problem. She locked the car, took a minute to stretch, and headed toward the gate.

The entrance was barred by a heavy steel pipe gate, which was hinged on one side and painted bright yellow. It remained locked except for service vehicles. On the other side of the barrier, old Petersham Road cut a swath twenty feet wide through the forest towards the old town of Dana, Massachusetts. Dana's common, rising one hundred seventy feet above the river valley, was the only town center that remained above the water line once the reserve was flooded. The old blacktop was crumbling but surprisingly intact after so many years.

It was two miles to the common. Then, a side road took her along the water's edge for another three. A loop trail circled back to the common, then back to the gate for an even ten miles. She was looking forward to it.

She was only a few hundred yards into the reserve when the fog thickened and visibility shortened to a mere fifteen feet. She considered turning back, but the joy of the run got the best of her and she pressed on. If she followed the pavement, the road would get her to the common and back at least. She tracked the road's edge as she ran. Then, something caught her eye. Off to the right, she spotted the entrance to a small dirt road branching off into the woods. It made her pull up to a full stop. Had that road been there before? Maybe she lost her bearings in the fog and was further along than she thought. The fog was even denser now, with visibility ten feet at best. Placing two large stones on the pavement to mark her place, she gingerly turned down the side road.

Walking now, she noticed that the quality of the road surface seemed to be improving from overgrown ruts to clean dirt and then to a comfortable packed gravel. It was definitely unusual for old roads in the reserve. The sound of her footsteps was eerily amplified by the fog. Stone walls started appearing at the road's edge. Hints of buildings emerged just beyond them, no more than faint outlines. She started to wonder if she'd somehow strayed outside of the park limits and into one of the local neighborhoods that surrounded the reservoir's boundary, but something didn't seem right.

When the fog began to lift slightly, what appeared before her was a small New England town from another era. She guessed 1930ish based on the pictures in the Visitor's Center that outlined the area's history. It looked oddly like she often imagined it. An uneasy feeling crept over her, and she was about to turn around when a small girl materialized on the road ahead. Michelle stopped mid-step.

"Miss?" a tiny voice called.

Michelle turned around to see if there was anyone else the girl might be referring to, but she was alone on the road. She turned back around. "Do you mean me, honey?"

"Yes."

As the girl stepped out of the mist, she was clearly wearing the short dress and ankle socks of a different era.

"Aaahhhh," Michelle took a cautious step back. "How can I help you?"

"I'm scared."

The girl appeared to be about five years old. Michelle immediately looked around for people or things of which to be afraid.

"Why are you scared, sweetie?" She was doing her best to not panic and not alarm the little girl—or whatever she was.

"Because they left me here." She began to tear up.

"Don't cry, honey. We'll figure it out." Michelle went into mommy mode. Again, she looked around. Maybe checking for safety, maybe looking for help, maybe making sure no one was watching on the chance that she was talking to herself. In any case, she saw no one.

"What's your name?" She squatted down to get on the girl's level.

"Grace Parker."

"Okay, Grace. Have you ever talked to anyone before?" She was trying desperately to figure out what was happening.

"I've never seen anyone before. You have funny clothes."

Michelle looked down at her running clothes, all Spandex and nylon, and smiled. "Yes, I do."

"You're not from around here. Are you one of those people from Boston who is making us move?"

"Not exactly, but maybe I can help. What seems to be the problem?"

"I'm stuck in the old well. That's why they left without me. They couldn't find me, and I couldn't get out."

Michelle's heart sank. "Where's the old well, Grace, honey?"

"Way out behind the blacksmith's shop. I was playing and fell in."

Michelle resisted the instinct to run immediately to the old well, wherever that was. "How can I help?"

"Please get me out of the well." Her lower lip puffed out. "And tell my sister I'm all right. It's not her fault."

Michelle had no idea what to say. Looking around for some kind of guidance, she found none. Even if she wanted to, how could she possibly help? The town of Dana had been abandoned eighty years ago. She turned back to see Grace's angelic eyes framed by delicate yellow curls looking pleadingly at her, and she simply couldn't say no.

"It's okay, Grace. I can help. But in order to help you, I need to get other people to help me. Do you understand?"

"You're going to leave me."

"Yes. I'm afraid so."

"Will you promise to come back?"

Michelle hesitated. A promise to a child, alive or not, was not to be taken lightly.

"Yes. I promise."

Standing up, she began backing away from Grace. The further she got, the thicker the fog, until Grace and the buildings were swallowed up again. She turned and ran back down the road until her feet landed on the familiar crumbling blacktop where her small pile of stones lay undisturbed. She turned to look back down the lane, but it was gone. She swiveled around to get her bearings. She recognized the old road that led down to the common—and back to the car.

"Okay. Done with my run for today," she said to no one, and ran straight for the parking lot.

She sat in her car for a few minutes replaying the encounter. Did she just have a conversation with a ghost child? It sure seemed that way. What was she supposed to do now? Call the police? Report a dead body in a well from eighty years ago? Go home and tell her husband

and teenage daughter? The last one seemed easiest and with the highest likelihood of not being locked up as a nut job, although she couldn't be entirely sure.

"Hello honey. I'm home," she called out as she entered the kitchen and dropped her keys in the bowl on the counter.

"You're back early. Everything okay?" Her husband, Jack, had a tone of concern in his voice.

"Well, not really, I think. I'm not sure. I met someone on the trail this morning and …"

Jack went straight to panic. "What? A guy? A crazy guy? Did he hurt you? Are you okay?" He grabbed her by the shoulders and was frantically looking her over, checking for injuries.

She shook him off irritably. "Yes, Jack! I'm fine. Calm down."

"Okay. Sorry." He took a step back and raised his hands in apology. "Occupational hazard." Jack was a crime and court reporter for several of the local papers. "What happened?"

At that moment her daughter, Marla, came around the corner into the kitchen looking for breakfast. On seeing Michelle, she asked, "Hey, Mom. Are you okay?"

Michelle snapped at her. "Yes! Why do you ask?"

Marla gave her the adolescent eye roll and huff. "Just looking a little stressed. That's all."

"Your mother encountered someone on the trail at Quabbin this morning."

"Really? A creep? A runner? A creepy runner?"

"A ghost."

Jack and Marla froze, speechless. Jack was the first to break the silence. "Okay, honey. You know that's impossible, right?"

Completely ignoring her father, Marla quickly jumped in. "Cool. What did it look like? Was it all see-through? Did it float? Oh my God! Did it talk to you?"

"Marla, there is no such thing as ghosts," her dad admonished.

"Dad. DUH. Obviously, something happened." Marla gestured toward her mother who was looking pale and unsettled.

"Oh, yeah, of course, come sit down." Jack led her to a kitchen chair. He and Marla took chairs on either side. "What happened?"

After hearing her tale, Marla was all about it. Jack was skeptical at best and kept insisting that they call the police and report a runaway girl. When his attempt to override the two women in his household got him nowhere, as usual, he agreed to accompany Marla on a little fact-finding excursion to the library to search old newspaper microfilm. Michelle headed to the Quabbin Reservoir Visitor's Center to see what kind of information they had about the old blacksmith shop or a missing girl. If they had any of the old maps, maybe one of them located the well in question. She wasn't sure what she would do then, but it would be one step at a time.

She was greeted by the ranger behind the information counter. "Good afternoon. My name is Dan. Can I help you with anything?"

"Yes. I'm interested in what things looked like before they flooded the reservoir, like maps of the towns, things like that."

"Well, we have some of those here in our archives. There's more information at the town hall in Belchertown. That's where all the records went when the towns were officially dissolved."

"Can I see Dana? I understand a lot of the town is still above the water line."

"That's right. We have them right here." He led her to a table with large plats, one for each town. He pulled out Dana. "Are you looking for something in particular?"

"I'm looking for the blacksmith shop. It was near the town common."

"That's right. There's a marker where the cellar hole is. You can walk down to it if you like. The trail starts at Gate 40."

"Yes. I know. I've been down there before. Say, have you ever heard a story about a small girl who went missing just before they closed the roads?"

"Can't say I have. But you can ask Betty Goodall. She was one of the last families to leave back in 1938. She just wrote a book about it called *Dana's Last Days*."

"Really? There are people still alive?"

"Sure. There's a whole community that keeps in touch and meets here once a year. They're getting pretty old, though. I think Betty is close to ninety. She'll be here in a few minutes. She's promoting her book today." The ranger looked up as the door opened. "And here she is." An elderly woman came through the door. She was pulling a small wheeled cart.

"Hello Ms. Betty. Let me help you with that." Dan hurried over to be of assistance.

"That's so kind of you, Daniel. Can you help Jenny bring in the books? She's parked right out front."

"I'm on it. And this woman here has a few questions for you about Dana. Why don't you have a seat over there, and Jenny and I will set up your table."

"Hello." Michelle ushered Ms. Betty over to a table and out of the line of traffic. "My name is Michelle. I'd love to talk to you about the last days of Dana if you have a few minutes."

"Certainly dear. What can I tell you?"

Michelle had concocted a slight variation on the truth. "I heard a story about the last few days of Dana when a five-year-old girl went missing. Do you recall anything about that?"

"That's just how old I was when my family left town. My memory might not be so good for other things, but I remember that time like it was yesterday. Everyone was so sad to leave. And angry too. My family got to stay to the very end because we were above the projected water line. Most people were long gone by then."

"Yes. I imagine so." Michelle tried to be patient. "Was there a missing girl back then?"

Betty thought for a minute. "Not that I recall," she shook her head. "Oh, no, wait. There *was* a girl. I haven't thought about her in years. She was a classmate of mine. Grace Parker was her name. It was quite the stir-up. Her family spent the day packing up the last of their possessions into the car. When they went looking for her, she was nowhere to be found. There was so much activity at the time, working men everywhere, big equipment destroying everything in sight. I was just a child myself then. I don't remember much else. We left that day ourselves. What makes you ask?"

Michelle hesitated for a long moment, deciding what to say next. "Do you believe in ghosts, Ms. Betty?"

Betty answered thoughtfully. "Let's just say that I believe there are things out there that I wouldn't believe," she paused, "Do you, Michelle?" Betty's eyes were sharp, almost piercing, as she waited for Michelle's reply.

Slowly, Michelle nodded. "I do now."

She went on to tell the story of the little girl in the fog while Dan and Jenny were busy arranging the book display. Realizing that no one would take the ghost story seriously, they quickly came up with an alternative. By the time the book table was arranged, the two conspirators had a better tale to tell.

"Daniel." Betty's voice was soft but commanding.

"Yes, Ms. Betty. What's the matter? Don't you like it?" He stood back so she could see the display table.

"It's fine, Daniel. Never mind that. Come over here and sit down."

Dan obediently complied. "Sure thing. What's up?"

"Well, Michelle has just poked at an old memory of mine, and I'm quite upset about it."

Daniel looked at Michelle with one eyebrow raised.

"No, no." Betty fussed at him. "I'm not upset with her. I'm upset with myself for not ever remembering, but it was so long ago, and I was just a child. I can't believe I've forgotten for all these years."

"Mom, what's wrong?" Jenny had joined the group and was unhappy to see her mother upset.

"Just before we left Dana, there was a girl that went missing, and I think I know where she is."

"What do you mean, Mom? You never said anything about it to me."

"I know. I just this minute remembered. I think she fell down the well behind the blacksmith shop. In fact, I know it. I remember that people were looking for her. I told my mother that I saw her playing out in the big field behind the forge, but everyone was so busy. She told me not to worry and finish packing my things. Then we left."

"I'm sure they found her, Mom."

"I don't think they did. I remember a few days later, my mother asking me where I had seen her last. Michelle here was just telling me that they never found her."

Dan turned to Michelle. "And how do you know about this?"

Michelle continued with the lie. "I had an old neighbor a few years ago who claimed to be from one of the other towns that got flooded. She remembered a story about a girl who went missing. There was a suspicion at the time that one of the men from out of town had something to do with it."

Betty jumped in before anyone could ask another question. "But I don't think so. I know there was an old well out in that field. We were always warned to stay away from there. And that's where I saw her. She's probably still there."

"Ms. Betty, I'm sure they looked everywhere for her," Dan explained. "There were plenty of police and rangers all over this place."

"I remember there being a terrible storm right after we moved. It might have covered up any evidence. No. I'm sure she's still there. Well, her body anyway. Poor little thing. We have to look, Daniel. We simply have to." Betty was wringing her hands now.

"Okay, Ms. Betty. Calm down. Let me think about what to do next."

At that moment, Jack and Marla arrived brandishing newspaper articles about the event, noting that a body was never discovered. When she was presumed dead a few years later, a marker went up in Quabbin Park Cemetery where human remains from the towns had been re-interred.

Daniel got on the phone to the Belchertown police who came over to hear Betty's story. They identified the location of the well on one of the maps in the Visitor's Center collection.

"I'll have to look into it, Ms. Betty. That's all I can say for sure." Officer Mahoney was shaking his head. "You know digging up around the reservoir is going to require permits from God right on down."

"I know you'll get it done, Bobby. Otherwise, I'll have to call your mother." She shook her finger at him.

He stood with his hands on his weapons belt and with the stern face of authority said, "I know you will, Ms. Betty. That's what really has me worried." He flashed her a grin and a wink.

"Seriously, though. I'll see what can be done and let you know. I'll keep Jen in the loop." He gave Jen a nod then headed out the door.

When Officer Mahoney determined that it was still an active unsolved case, he began working the phones. It took a week and a half to get the permits—record time considering all the red tape. Not surprisingly, when you're talking about the remains of a child, no matter how long ago, people make things happen. The reservoir authority didn't have any complaints as long as it was more than a hundred feet from the water's edge and they didn't have to pay for it. Belchertown agreed to absorb the cost but wanted the police to oversee the excavation. The state police would send a representative but their backlog of cold case files meant they wouldn't put any time into it for several months. In the event that a body turned up, the Springfield coroner was their best bet.

Two weeks later, a large group arrived to excavate the well. Present were a state police captain, Officer Mahoney, a city councilman up for re-election, the state fish and game director, a representative from the water resource management office, a public works supervisor, a heavy equipment operator with a backhoe, and two guys with shovels. Mostly everyone stood around and watched the two guys with shovels do all the work. Eventually, the skeleton of a small girl was discovered and assumed to be that of Grace Parker. Dr. Ben Jefferson, from the Springfield coroner's office, determined that the injuries were consistent with a fall, and the cause of death was presumed to be accidental.

There was enough information to track the family to Schenectady, NY, where Grace's sister, Pearl, now ninety-three, was living with her daughter. The family came down, and her remains were interred in the Quabbin Memorial Cemetery where her existing marker had been amended to reflect the actual date of death, June 3, 1938.

"Pearl?" Michelle tapped her on the shoulder as she sat at the graveside after the service. "Can I have a minute of your time?"

"Certainly dear. I understand you're involved in this somehow, and I thank you."

She sat down beside her in a chair vacated by a family member. "Oh, I'm happy I could help. There is one more thing, though."

Michelle had decided on another white lie to ease the conversation along.

"I had a dream last night, and Grace was in it. She asked me to tell you that it wasn't your fault." Michelle waited for a response.

Pearl sat quietly for a moment as tears filled her eyes. "Thank you for that, dear. It's been a burden to carry it all these years. I forgave myself a long time ago but not quite all the way. It's a blessing to know Grace forgave me too. You see, I was supposed to be watching her that day. I turned my back for a minute, and she was gone. That's how she was, always running here and there."

"It must have been a crazy time."

"We spent two days looking for her, but then we had to go. They were tearing our house down. We spent the next few years hoping she'd turn up somehow, somewhere. After that we started hoping that she died quickly, not at the hands of some criminal like a few were suggesting. Now, I'll say she died playing."

Michelle continued to run her favorite loop at Quabbin Reservoir. On those rainy, overcast days, she secretly hoped the town would appear again.

SEEING

Phyllis Cochran

"Just see for yourself," Suzy whispered to me.

I turned away reluctantly.

What could she see—blind to my eyes;

Yet these words caused my faith to rise.

Did she see perfectly clear

While only through her was I able to hear?

Did God will our children early to die

Leaving their families alone to cry?

Could a God who created sky and sea

Not care about how parents grieve?

Words from the Bible came to mind:

"Seek me first and you will find."

Who is this God who cares to be sought?

In the dark of night, I asked distraught.

Scriptures I read filled me with woe

With God's only son hung dying, slow.

The Father Almighty knows of our loss:

He watched His son, Jesus, die on the cross.

God cares about life, but also death.

He created us beings, breathed into us breath

Knowing one day we might turn Him away

Like the 99th sheep, could each go astray?

He loved us enough to watch His son die,

He shares in our sorrow, our tears He will dry.

Comfort each other with thoughts like these.

Remember often to fall on your knees.

Our children live on through eternal love

With God in Heaven, they watch from above.

For a child shall lead them, the Bible does say,

Just see for yourself—Suzy pointed the way.

VIEWS OF THE VALLEY
Jon Bishop

I'm at the bottom,

the lull, the low green crater,

looking at the top,

staring at this behemoth—

this grey, sleeping, jagged face,

crowned with clouds.

I can't climb it, because it bursts

from the ground

and shoots straight into the sky,

piercing the blue;

and if I did try

to climb it,

I'd fall—

shatter into a million pieces;

my broken body would spread

like feed

for the animals and the green.

That would give you something to see,

because right now you're up there,

looking down, breathing in—

smiling wide at the swaying emerald sea,

loving the valley.

You say it's picturesque,

but you don't see me

stranded at the bottom—

broken.

FACTORY GIRLS: BRAVERY

Ruth DeAmicis

Many ways to bravery.

Tired, so tired. At 3 pm on a Friday afternoon, there was little to look forward to even as the weekend loomed.

Ha.

Her mind laughed; see that joke right there? Looming indeed.

Emily had agreed to a half shift tomorrow. Only 6 to noon.

Still, she could have some time for herself.

She followed the crowd of other factory girls down the dusty lane, her head down, watching her feet scuff newly fallen leaves. A girl ahead was pushed off the path to peals of laughter.

"You wouldn't! Belle! That is scandalous!"

The girl in question put hands to hips and shot back, "And why the devil not? We look at one another, and smile, and duck, and smile, and it goes nowhere. I will speak first. I will."

Her friends shrieked.

Belle rejoined the group, and the laughter continued.

Em watched them go, wondering at their energy and freedom with one another. She didn't know how to do that, how to fit into that world.

Two young workers ran by, their shouts of joy at being out of work and into the world were like a raven's sharp caw.

She shrank away and watched them as they caught up to the gaggle of factory girls and danced backwards, pulling their caps off their heads and grinning.

"Ladies," shouted the taller one. "How fair you all are, how fair. Might you be attending Doyle's this eve?"

One tall girl in the center of the group tossed her blonde head.

"You invitin' Charles Bennett? You invitin'?"

He looked at her as he continued his saucy backwards skip.

"You Maureen? Absolutely. Will I see you there?"

She smiled, a slow wicked grin, "Maybe…"

The boys waved and ran on, the girls laughed more, closing ranks. Emily continued on alone.

The boarding house rang with giggles and calls as the young women climbed the narrow, enclosed stairs to the second and third floor dormitories. The long narrow rooms ran the width of the house, with small beds tucked under the eaves, trunks placed at the foot of each; a few hooks installed on the horsehair plaster walls between. Clothing hung from the hooks, a motley collection of skirts and overblouses, capes and bonnets. Each girl was allotted two, but somehow some seemed to have more than others.

Emily scurried to her corner cot at the furthest edge of the room. She sat on the small bed and watched the others, who seemed eager to change clothes and leave again.

Annie Bateman sat across from her, "Will you come out tonight, Em?"

She shook her head.

"I need to send the money home, not spend it," Em said.

Annie smiled her quiet smile, "I send most of mine away too, but I keep back a bit for my own."

"I cannot, they need it so."

Emily brought to mind her parents and the struggle on the bare rock Maine farm. The drought had shortened the season for two years, leaving her family not only nothing to sell, but nothing to eat. It was why she had come south in the first place. Women were needed in the mills.

"I work tomorrow too. Will you take my pay to the post office for me? I will address the envelope…"

"Of course I will, of course. But Em, do come out for a bit, you must have more than just work to think about," Annie reached for her hand.

But Em pulled back, shaking her head.

"No. I have a book. I shall sit downstairs I think, in the parlor where it's cooler. I will enjoy that."

Annie shook her head.

"I cannot make you, of course, but you are old before your time, Miss Em. Leave the envelope with me in the morning; I shall take care of it for you."

Em allowed herself a smile. Annie was close to being a friend, sharing the closest cot to hers and speaking often. She did seem to care and was willing to be helpful. Em thought she really should be friendly back.

"Thank you Annie, I do appreciate it. I think I am going to rest a bit, if the noise doesn't get too bad." She laid herself back on the small bed, covering her eyes with her arm; a clear signal to Annie to leave.

Annie took the hint, and she rummaged through her trunk for a clean blouse—hoping she could get a chance to iron it with so many others also trying to get gussied up for the night.

Several girls tussled in the doorway, laughing about getting down to the washhouse first, hoping to get a chance at warm water for a wash; it was only in fun though, as they all flounced down the steps together.

It left the stuffy attic room strangely silent.

Em took her arm away from her face and looked around. Clothes were strewn over beds, trunks hung open, a spill of talcum was scattered over the floor near the door. It had been a woman whirlwind.

She tried turning her back to it all and facing the wall, ignoring what she knew was there, but her own conscience wouldn't let her relax.

With a sigh, she got up and began straightening. Knowing who slept where, and whose belongings were whose, she folded, straightened, and put away everything. If she were uncertain, she left the folded clothes on the end of the bed rather than into a trunk, just in case she was wrong. She found the broom and swept up the talc.

Looking about, she felt a sense of relief.

She did like the others, but they frightened her. She didn't know how they could be so free with one another, so easily talk among themselves, so easily fit together.

It was a mystery.

She debated lying down again, but decided to take her book downstairs instead. There was no formal dinner on Friday and Saturday nights, so Em looked for the catch-as-you-can meal Mrs. Marshall always left out. Many of the others ate out as part of the evening festivities.

Some came home with no money left of the wages, even though they had just been paid.

And it had been nearly $10. A princely sum. Whatever did they spend it on, she wondered.

Mrs. Marshall was seated in the parlor herself, some needlework in her hands and a small smile on her old face. She listened to the women in her charge laughing and carrying on outside in the washhouse.

It brought back memories of being a young woman herself. Not so many, many years ago, she had been a weaver too. Actually, Mrs. Marshall had a loom at home for many years, but had been convinced to come work at a factory as it paid more than the piecework she had been doing for the same company at home.

It had been a challenge to leave her home and work outside. She could no longer stop for a bit and start supper, or check on her children, or work later at night if she wanted to. Now, it was only the "shop" and only when she was there.

She'd sold her home loom.

She missed it actually. She had been a good weaver, but she began to slow down, not able to keep up with new, faster machines. On top of that, when her Charlie died and her children were all out working, the factor had offered her this position at the single women's boarding house. He gave her a home, charged her with keeping the young women "in line," and even gave her a small wage and paid for some upkeep.

The women paid for board and that paid for the food; she stretched the income so the meals were filling and good.

Her single helper did the heavy cleaning and laundry, and had a room in the house too, behind the kitchen.

It worked for them all. The women all felt safe in the environment; no men were allowed and Mrs. Marshall stuck to that single rule passionately. If a girl got involved, she had to meet her "fella" somewhere else, not at the house. While Mrs. Marshall had a safe home as she aged, and her "girls" had a safe home away from home, they all felt like a small family.

Which of course was why Friday and Saturday nights were such a treat for the girls. It was a chance to meet and talk to the "fellas" outside of the work environment—to be single girls for a while and, in this new modern age, to be free to encourage a little flirtation.

Em came in with her book while munching on bread and honey. Mrs. Marshall looked up and pursed her lips.

"You are not going out?" she asked.

Em shook her head, her mouth full, then used the napkin she'd brought with her to wipe away the sticky honey around her lips.

"No, not this week," she said.

Mrs. Marshall paused, not wanting to be sharp, but concerned this little mouse was too timid.

"Has anyone been cruel or mistreated you here, Emily? Have you been made to feel unwelcome?"

Em was surprised by the questions.

"Why, no, not at all. Everyone has been quite lovely Mrs. Marshall. Quite."

"You don't seem to get on with them, is all. You seem to stay by yourself so much." The older woman frowned, her concern very real.

Em hadn't thought anyone would notice her reticence, except maybe Annie, why would they? She was nothing to anyone here, but apparently, she was wrong.

"I truly am very happy, Mrs. Marshall. Things are just fine. I send my money home and prefer not to party, is all. The girls have invited me; I have chosen not to go," Emily explained.

But Mrs. Marshall, much as Annie, did not think the answer was enough.

"You really should go out on occasion; it is more than just the 'party' as you say. It's a chance to get to know the others outside of work. You can't do that if you don't go, there isn't any other time to do it, not really," said Mrs. Marshall. She smiled as she encouraged Em.

Em sighed. Maybe it needed to happen, but how she couldn't fathom. She could stick by Annie, she supposed, if Annie wouldn't mind too much.

"All right, you and everyone else seem to think I need to stop being a hermit, though I am perfectly happy so," Em shrugged away. "So I'll consider it, will that do?"

"Oh Emily, please, yes. Just consider it, that is not a demand."

But somehow, it felt like it.

———————

The next morning, as Emily put together her post for Annie to take, she added in her weekly note that she would be saving a couple dollars for herself in the future. She feared her family would not be happy about that, but they would not answer her letter right away. She could do it for this week at least.

As she left for the half day shift, she told Annie what she had done.

"I will go with you tonight, if I may…" she was hesitant to ask.

But she shouldn't have worried, Annie threw her arms around her in a hug.

"How marvelous! I am so glad! We shall have a ripping good time, and I know just where to go!" Annie laughed at Emily's crestfallen face.

"Oh, don't worry, I won't make a fallen woman of you!"

"I just, I don't know…"

Annie sobered up.

"Emily, it's all right. We'll go slow, just a cup of tea with some of the others; maybe stop to see some of the things to see. You don't have to sing and dance to have a good time," Annie winked.

Emily was horrified.

"I don't have to, do I?"

"Of course not. You really are so easy to get going, aren't you? Hurry home, I'll help you choose clothes."

And Annie was off to visit with others, gathering up Emily's letter with her own as she left.

When Emily returned home after having been kept late by the overseer who had hoped to finish a run of the stock, Annie was already dressed in a full dark green skirt and pale pink blouse with her hair pulled up in a dainty bun, and threaded with a pink ribbon.

"Oh, I am so glad you are home. I have a gift for you!"

Annie pulled a pale green blouse from behind her back.

"I bought the pink and the green to go with this skirt, but I don't like this green one after all, so I am going to give it to you. Do you have a skirt it will go with?"

"I have a black skirt…"

"Perfect! Does it need ironing?"

"Probably, and I need a bath."

"You go to the washhouse, I will take care of the clothes, get me your skirt."

Emily rummaged in her trunk, pulling out a wool skirt made with gores to give it shape. It also had a soutache trim around the bottom.

"That is lovely," said Annie, taking it from her.

Emily smiled. "I made it. I saw something similar on someone and, well, I just made it."

"But that is marvelous! That is talent, Miss Em! Not everyone can do that!"

"It isn't anything."

"But it is, I could never just see something I like and figure out how to make it. That is hard to do," Annie held the skirt up. "This is well made."

Em was embarrassed, she ducked her head, grabbed for her toweling and rushed out—hoping Annie would take the hint and not continue the praise. It felt ... wrong to Emily. She wasn't worthy of it.

The bath was a quick one. Others wanted in as well, and the hot water was kept boiling to keep refreshing the tub. She didn't wash her hair, that was a production in itself, and perhaps she would do that tomorrow. Now, she rushed back upstairs, wondering if she could grab a bite to eat here so she wouldn't have to find food later.

But in the end, she left with Annie, dressed in the green and black and with Annie's deft touch to her hair. It felt awkward to be out with the others, and she left resolved.

Walking up the street with an entire crowd of women later, Em kept on the inside of the group, afraid of the many, many people about her. It seemed the entire town was out on the street tonight. People kept breaking off from her group to enter the stores or restaurants, a small pub took some, and a dry goods store a few more. Soon she, Annie, and two others were the only ones left. Taking her arm, Annie turned Em to look across the street.

"See that little shop there? That's Richardson's Tea Shop. We can go there, it's quieter, and small. Is that all right?"

Em smiled. "Perfect. Just perfect."

With that, Annie called to the others as she led Em away, just to let them know they were leaving. Dodging knots of other young people milling the streets, Annie eventually brought Em into the small room set with five little tables and chairs. They took a table near the windows.

Em was relieved to be away from the overwhelming noise of the street. She looked around at the small space. She admired the high tin ceiling with its embossed pattern, the counter across the way with a row of tin kettles steaming away on small coal fired stove tops. A round woman with a crisp white apron came over.

"Tea, loveys?"

Annie winked at Em.

"Yes, please. And scones, with the clotted cream and the raspberry jam please."

Em had no idea what Annie had asked for, but trusted it would be good.

She watched out the window, amazed as groups of people came together, talked, made different groups, and moved away. The movement and progression was a dance. How did that happen?

The woman came back and set down the cups, a plate of little round pastries, and a tray with the jam and cream in matching dishes.

She watched Annie doctor her pastry. Em did the same, and moaned at the first bite. Heaven.

"What is this?"

"Scone. From England I think. Isn't it good?"

Outside, a fight had broken out. Em jumped as the loud voices chimed through the windows. She watched two young men rolling around on the dirt street, cuffing at one another. Watching, proud of herself, was the girl named Belle who had been so bold yesterday. A third boy, bigger than others, entered the fray. He pulled the two fighters up and separated them. He shook them sharply like a terrier with rats. Em couldn't hear what he said, but apparently he convinced the two to give up the scuffle.

Belle didn't look pleased that her "beau" was no longer fighting over her. She turned with her friends and left.

The three boys in the middle of the road turned to one another. The two fighters shook hands, grinned at one another, and took off together. The remaining boy watched them go and shook his head. To Em's surprise, he turned to the tea shop.

Em shrank back, thinking such a big fellow was scary.

He came in, ducking a little at the doorway, though actually that may have been a reflex, as his head cleared the jamb easily. He looked around, and took the table next to Annie and Em. He dusted his hands off on his canvas trousers. He smiled at Annie, who smiled back.

"Hello, Hank."

"Annie, how be ya?"

"Good, I'm good. Bit of a bother there?"

Hank shrugged. "Just a bit of a tussle. No harm." He asked the proprietor for strong tea, and glanced at Em, who shrank back.

"Hank, this is Em, my friend," Annie introduced them.

Hank lowered his chin, seeming to try to make himself smaller, "How do, Miss Em."

Em smiled, he wasn't so bad after all. He reminded her a bit of her cousin Tommy, a similarly large boy, who felt out of place with his size.

"Hello," she said.

They sat silently. No one seemed to know what to say next. Annie finally cleared her throat and said, "would you care to move your chair here? Join us?"

A slow smile showing clean, even teeth beamed from Hank. What a thing to notice, Em thought.

He moved his chair, bringing his mug of strong tea, and faced out the window. They sat in silence again. Again, Annie took the lead.

"Where is it you work at the mill?" Annie asked. "I see you about, but …"

"I do the bobbins. I calibrate and reset the bobbins before your looms," he said.

"Ah, so not in our rooms then. But I have seen you."

"Yah. Sometimes I need to come in and get back a bobbin if it didn't wind proper. So I do come to the looms sometimes."

Em looked at his big, strong hands. He would need strong hands to pull and stop spinning bobbins. Centrifugal force sometimes kept them going even after a machine stopped. And he must be smart. Calculating the machines to do the math to make them wind proper was challenging.

Her job was much easier in comparison. She wanted to ask him about that, and she found her voice.

"So do you have to calculate while they are winding? Do you have to redo them if they aren't winding right?" She was a bit abashed that she was brave enough to ask.

But Hank smiled gently, seeming to know she was winding up her courage with her question.

He answered with a low, gentle voice, encouraging her.

They sat there for two hours, talking about many things — they had much in common: families, farms, and small lives. Also, they had similar backgrounds and a love of books.

Hank and Em found it easy to talk to one another, not noticing at all when Annie said quietly that she had to meet someone else and left. Only when Hank asked if he could walk her home as the proprietor began closing up her little shop, did Em realize how long it had been.

"Oh, oh my," she startled, looking around.

Hank smiled his slow, quiet smile. He had found a partner here, someone so like him. He was amazed: a reader, a thinker. She was not interested in the high life, like many of his coworkers, after the long hours of work. He wanted to be sure she would feel as if he was worthy of seeing him as, at least, a friend.

"May I walk you back to Mrs. Marshall's?" He said. "I want to be sure you are home safe. And I would like to see you again. I want to bring you that book I told you about. I think you would enjoy it."

Em smiled. Yes. This gentle giant was not at all what she had expected. She felt very safe with him. She wanted to know him better, if only as a friend. She was willing to see him again and talk about books, and people, and the world.

"We could meet at the park tomorrow?" she offered.

"Yes, we could. I work at four, to set up for Monday morning. Is two a good time for you?"

We could, she thought, we could do that. And I will be brave.

She nodded and held out her hand to be helped from her chair. Hank took her hand, then offered his arm. He towered above her, at least a foot taller. He moved slowly, keeping his pace alongside hers as they turned down the street.

The crowds didn't seem as big or loud with him at her side. She looked at him. She looked at the people on the street.

Sometimes bravery is just who you're with, isn't it?

TULLYFINE MOUNTAIN WOMAN

Kathleen Bennett

If a calendar contains my lifespan,

August would reveal where I am.

Here I sit and contemplate this day

Mid-month, among a year past half way,

Vernal spirit within avows the parallel

Of glorious heights soaring from the dell.

My own Spring has come and departed,

Graciously unfinished in what it has started.

What could be any sweeter than dew-drenched berries,

Or serene, serenading tunes the songbirds carry?

Sweeter yet, the vista from where I sit

Luscious greenery—sumptuous, exquisite.

Late noon sun beams a drowsy haze,

Hovering Mount Tully upon which I gaze.

The river below babbles

Along sun-speckled travels…

Let me unravel, relish the calm

This peaceful mid-August day, my balm.

If only one thing I can know for sure,

The whispers of time render the body mature.

And so, even though

The days hereafter grow shorter and cold,

I delight

In the height of a lovely season growing old.

TO DESCRIBE NEW ENGLAND AUTUMN TO A COSTA RICAN
Eileen Kennedy

The season arrives smashed,

fall, summer, spring, and winter at once.

The day starts a cotton ball patch of wet fog and burns off

a whirling red and orange chameleon. The afternoon

a cloudless sky lens for the searing sun clear as vodka.

Holding the gold-leafed rays in my hands,

I give it to them. So like their afternoon,

this light they would understand,

offering up fragrances of coconut-like apple pulp.

Not passiflora in pistils, but fixed pine and decaying leaves.

Not voluptuous cockatoos, but geese and ducks offering

slow steady migration formations.

Not a gentle breeze, but the cold code

of this one-time season. The sun

that sets here has no point. Winter arrives

on the shoulders of the dusk

a dark stole clothing the night.

The still surface of the lake

a moon canvas for glistening paths.

This doesn't belong to me.

There are no words to tell it in Spanish or English.

They align con simpatico: night lake human moon beast.

Published in Compass Roads: A Dispatch from Paradise/Poems about the Pioneer Valley, edited by Jane Yolen and the Straw Dogs Writer's Guild, Leveller's Press Spring 2018.

CHAOS WITH A CHANCE OF SILENCE

Jennifer Delozier

Waiting for precious life.

Burdens tumbling giving strife

Are not waiting for the light.

High on the worldview,

mud-like flooded rivers flow,

drowning hearts in the swell.

Push-button fast food

aligning with solar goods?

Heads hang in despair,

There's poison in the air.

Silence no longer exists.

The weight of terror reigns.

They are arguing,

"Wait," they mumble under their breath,

"Describe our suffering."

Horns and sirens blow

beneath Greenfield's traffic.

Where has the quiet been?

On the far side now,

joy waiting for all us people.

A silent conception of peace.

PUZZLES

Diana Lynne Norman

Locked behind the formidable doors, I am watched like a hawk and treated with powerful medications—aimed to make me "well." I am aware that my voice has been hushed by their chemicals, but it is still magnified in my mind. My thoughts, my opinions, random ideas are streaming through my still remaining blaring cognizance. The cognitions that tumble in my awareness are excruciating—protesting the preposterous realities that I observe.

Thankfully, scribbling with a dull golf pencil on copier paper offers slight relief. As I write, the filled pages drift like autumnal leaves, around my feet, the table, the floor. My words make sense now … *Whose bright idea was it to offer puzzles in psych wards?*

Did you know that science has proven puzzle books—word searches, crosswords and coloring books—beneficial to people with mental illnesses? Remarkable, I'll be cured soon! Actually, I've never read one study postulating their beneficial applicability in mental health treatment. But, based on their prevalence on each ward to which I've been admitted, I suppose at least *someone* believes they're therapeutic in some way. Admittedly, it is a method to help patients divert their minds from their troubles or at the very least circumvent boredom.

I make a concerted effort to avoid these books like the plague. My stays on these secure units are typically mandatory and as the result of some unstable mood state augmented by extreme irritability. In particular, these books exasperate the hell out of me when I am "well"—let alone when I am truly not.

Having endured several stints in places like this one, I've come to the realization that every ward saves stacks and stacks of old magazines and boxes and boxes of old puzzles. My guess is that this clutter-mess has been donated over the years. All the individuals who've ever been in charge of such facilities seem to experience difficulty throwing anything of such pristine value away. Instead of seeking order, the stacks continue to accumulate.

These old magazines are not worth the paper they were printed on. Instead, they serve to provide additional vexation by their encumbering existence. Having a mental health label doesn't necessarily imply patients desire to read garbage! I understand creating collages from these magazines is a *vital* and *important* part of an art group, but only a tiny portion of these magazines would be more than adequate to create hundreds of collages for a myriad of patients!

So perhaps I might be cured with the copious games with which numerous shelves in the activity rooms are unfailingly laden. These boxed amusements are all from the 1980s or before. Some classics never die. Apparently, having one or two pieces missing, rendering the activity unplayable, appears an insufficient reason for discarding them. Instead, they're jumbled on the shelves, teasing and testing like cruel tormentors. Is this malicious aspect of ward life masquerading as a methodological cure?

Boxed jigsaw puzzles far overshadow all contenders as the root of all evil in the mental health field. Perhaps they are so prevalent on these secure Behavioral Health Units as a method to test patients' coping strategies when insanity strikes. An individual might be evaluated as they work on puzzles—especially when, after hours and hours spent fitting the tiniest of pieces together, it is discovered that the puzzle is incomplete.

It would be logical to most of us—even those of us who actually require treatment here behind the locked doors—to toss the incomplete puzzle. Instead, it is placed deliberately back on the shelf wickedly poised to lure another unsuspecting patient.

And this idiocy is supposed to help my irritability, my sanity?

A tiny, smooth, white pill.

Can restore inner tranquility.

A sense of fulfilment.

Is that a lesson I'm supposed to learn?

Have I solved the puzzle?

A CACOPHONY OF SILENCE

Jan VanVaerenewyck

Early on a Saturday morning, the distant Route 2 traffic can be mistaken for the sounds of waves. I imagine the saltiness of ocean air, the ebb and flow of weekend travelers sailing on the west wind. My mind hears these sounds, tells me it is quiet. But it is a constant hum.

It is seldom silent now. There is a thrum in the air: furnaces, washing machines, cars, computers, and airplanes. I don't think most people are comfortable with silence. It is a void to fill with music, television, or conversation. Running is a lone act, yet the runners are plugged into their phones—listening to music, podcasts, even books. Do we avoid being alone with our thoughts?

Though there is silence that we love: that blessed moment after the wailing baby finds the nipple of a breast or bottle. Or when the winter clouds, thick and gray, muffle all sound, and the first snowflakes drifts onto an upturned face. There is that moment of stillness on a spring morning, right before dawn. The breeze rises, the music begins. A cacophony of feathered instruments blends melodies into a morning symphony.

The absence of sound can create a sad silence. After the twin towers were bombed, there was silence in the skies. No drone of engines shifting overhead. A reminder of the lives lost, and a profound shock to the American way of life. Then it was back to noise as usual.

In the end, there is the silence around the bed as sons and daughters gather, listening to each breath their father takes. They don't speak, their sibling banter dies in their throats. Soon the focus shifts from listening to the harsh respirations to measuring the increasing length between breaths. In silence they count as they did as children:

Mississippi-one, Mississippi-two. They do not look at each other, but at the shallow rise and fall of their father's chest. Until there is only silence.

LISTEN TO THE NIGHT
Michael Young

The subtle sounds of rain,

summer falling down.

Peepers sang of spring,

pond and tree.

Now crickets signal change of seasons—

Strike the set!

Coyote insinuates into my sleep.

First, her call,

then her dream presence

"She's up the slope!"

Some creature strange

let out a cry between house and wood.

There's a message there somewhere.

Fauna creeps through flora.

Field fog morning

witnesses deer paths

down the hedgerow,

underneath the hayfield fence.

Silent circle beds

pressed in tall grasses.

Sure signs

the world doesn't

stop the show

while we snooze.

A SUMMER WALK

Kay Deans

Air hangs heavy on my shoulders

while clouds make the heat bearable.

Thunder rolls in the distance,

a storm to the south moving away.

My joints creak with inactivity,

but a faint breeze grows stronger and

pulls me into the road for a walk.

A horsefly circles my head.

I wave my arms and she retreats,

but she comes back.

I swat at her, shake my head,

raise my arms …

She is persistent

and so am I.

We are passing our sheep field where

there are many animals and she could feast.

She does not need me.

What does she want?

There is plenty of space, so

we could share, and walk in peace.

But with her incessant tormenting

my arms tire, my shoulders ache,

beads of sweat roll down my face and neck.

The horsefly wins.

I go home, sit in a chair

and wallow in my misery.

A flash of light and the house shakes with

a crack of thunder,

my body vibrating with it.

Then a deluge begins.

The horsefly was my savior.

VOICES

Steven Michaels

Julia hadn't been in the hospital very long, or at least, it didn't feel that long. People told her she had been there for several months. Thankfully, the coma had shortened the sensation, and so Julia was convinced she could resume her normal life as if the accident had never happened. She had suffered no signs of amnesia and all her vitals seemed improving. Within another three weeks, she would be free to go home. But to what?

Julia lived alone in a most Eleanor-Rigby way. She sometimes chuckled to herself when the song came on the radio. She most certainly did *not* keep a face in a jar by the door—still, the idea of purchasing some petrified remains to keep as a literal metaphor intrigued her every time the line echoed in her mind.

When asked about her recent coma by nurses who had never experienced administering to a coma patient, Julia replied it was a most pleasant interlude.

"I'm sure your family is relieved," they would say at the close of every conversation.

And Julia never had the heart to say that she had none.

At last Julia was released. She returned to her one bedroom apartment with a nearly non-existent cat. She delighted in the cliche of crazy cat lady, although having one was enough for her. Naturally, the cat she chose was more aloof than she; the only evidence of him living there could be found in a litter box along with a trail of food leading out onto the fire escape. He was a survivor, much like herself. The fact that no one needed to care for him during her coma earned him reverent respect and admiration. And if she could remember what color or type he was, she would have descended upon any feline bearing his resemblance with one hundred affectionate kisses.

That was the trouble with being alone: the yearning to send forth love. Even in her coma, she could remember the urgings to send forth a message of some kind. True, the coma had felt brief, but perhaps that was because she had been in a virtual coma her whole life.

One afternoon, a few days after getting settled back home, she heard them.

Voices.

"Look at her ... she's so beautiful ..."

It was a man's voice.

"I just love to watch her sleep ..."

At night, the voice would echo in her brain, as an image of a teal cloth shifted just beyond her peripheral.

"Can't believe this chick got hit by a bus ..."

Julia wasn't sure what to think, but eventually it became apparent: these were voices she heard while in a coma.

"Her vitals seem to be stable ..."

This had the lilt of an authorative woman. Her doctor? Or just some tired nurse?

"I don't want to sleep in no room with a vegetable!"

This came as growl from an angry old man, who only ever shouted once and was gone.

"Ella se ve muy tranquila..."

A soft voice murmured, as if in prayer, while a swirling mop handle danced off to Julia's left.

But the man's voice continued to stand out the most.

"Chick got hit by a bus … Look at her … she's so beautiful … I just love to watch her sleep…."

Much like the non-existent cat who was in and out of her apartment, Julia's curiosity began to pique. Did she actually have an admirer? Nonsense. She was mishearing the voice. But in her loneliness, the repeated phrases soothed her.

"It's a miracle … She has no idea how much I love her …"

This phrase was too hard to ignore. But how could she know who the man was? Introverts like Julia didn't go barging into people's workplaces, let alone hospitals to ask men out on a date. And wouldn't *he* call upon her if he was so infatuated? Then again, maybe it was frowned upon due to some patient-doctor regulation.

But why did he say these things out loud? Who was he talking to? Why didn't he just address her.

Then:

"You awake baby girl? I've only got eyes for you …"

Damn it. Her lonely heart swooned as this male baritone sang these words in her ear. She at least had to find out if the man existed.

Several weeks later Julia returned to the hospital, unsure of how to ask the front desk about a sexy male nurse who whispered to her in the night. Slowly, she walked up to the receptionist at the ward where she had been.

"Oh hello. Julie, was it? Are you here for some sort of follow up?" asked the woman who earned special points for getting Julia's name nearly right.

"No, I, um, er, well …" began Julia, before growing pale.

"Oh dear, I'm sorry. You were in that coma, weren't you? Did you forget something? I didn't think you had amnesia. Wait, do you want me to call a doctor?"

"No, no. Well, maybe. Is there a doctor whose voice register is slightly, um …"

Julia stopped, realizing how crazy that sounded as the receptionist looked at her blankly.

"I'm sorry. Do you want me to call you a doctor?

Long pause.

"Yes …"

The receptionist picked up the phone.

"I have that coma patient from a few weeks ago here; she seems disoriented. Should I call down to emergency or what?"

"Nevermind. I can see you're busy. I was just, just …"

"Listen, honey, part of my job is to worry about people. Go ahead and have a seat, and I'll get someone to see you."

Julia sat down on a nearby chair. Its plastic arms enveloped her. She noticed another chair that was slightly larger than hers. She wasn't a petite person, and certainly the chair she had chosen wasn't too confining; however, as she was feeling emotionally uncomfortable, she pondered moving to the more spacious chair, whose plastic arms weren't so close to her midsection. Perhaps she shouldn't have come here at all. She shifted her weight slightly and had nearly made up her mind to leave when a very attractive man in scrubs came towards her.

Surely, the universe isn't this generous, she thought.

He stopped and looked at her.

"Julia Kosinski?" he asked in a very familiar tone.

"Yes, well, no, it's pronounced Kozinska."

"Very cool," he said smoothly. "I'm Dr. Lance. Listen, I hope you're doing okay. I visited you a couple times while doing my residency here."

Julia's heart quickened, and she looked pale.

"So, are you okay?" he inquired. "You want me to take your vitals?"

"No, er, no ... Maybe. Goodness, it seems so hot in here."

"Try to stay calm. I got a crash cart on the ready, but I don't think you'll need it," he uttered softly and reassuringly.

"No, probably not," breathed Julia, feeling the urge to chuckle and barf.

"Oh good, you're coming around, but do you mind if I take your pulse, just in case?"

He gently picked up her arm and looked at his watch. He was definitely a young doctor; maybe a month or two into his residency as he mentioned. Julia hadn't much considered men younger than herself, but in truth she didn't always consider people at all. She realized how ridiculous this all was. She shouldn't be infatuated with this stranger because of some sweet nothings that could very easily be dismissed as a dream.

"Well, your heart's definitely racing. Any idea what caused this? Is that why you came in?" he asked.

Julia wasn't ready to answer honestly.

"No, but I have been—" She stopped. Would they put her in the mental ward if she confessed to hearing voices and stalking this poor man? As her eyes wandered away from him, she noticed the ring.

"You're married?" she asked, slightly annoyed.

"Yeah, I met her my first year of college. We even have a daughter."

A daughter? Way to go, Universe! thought Julia. *Why are all the handsome, successful men such creeps? I shouldn't feel guilty, should I? He's the one with the coma patient fetish! Uck!*

"I'm sorry. Did you want to say something?" asked Dr. Lance, noticing the sudden look of disgust on her face.

Embarrassed, Julia breathed hard.

"Nevermind, I can just go right? Do I have to check out or something? What am I saying? I'm not even a patient here anymore. I have to go."

"Wait, Julia. I want to help you. And I have a confession to make."

Holy Father McKenzie! she thought. *What is happening?*

"I probably shouldn't be telling you this, but you seem like a nice person. I mean, you were asleep, so how much of a jerk could anyone be? Anyway, I, uh, during my overnights, I would go into your room to video chat with my wife so I could see my newborn baby girl. My late hours made it hard for me, and I just couldn't be away from her … new dad jitters, I guess. I hope it didn't disturbed you, so I apologize if it did. Anyway, I thought you should know … I felt really bad about using your room, but I was on call, and it was the quietest room I could find … I think I did my best to treat you while I made those calls. But hey, I'm still learning. So … are we cool?"

The way he said this made it clear he was still very young; he had basically addressed her like she was the teacher, and he had unintentionally acted up in class. Julia just shook her head at her own stupidity.

"Yeah, yeah," breathed Julia. "As cool as … a cat. I'm gonna go."

He tilted his head in confusion; then shrugged it off and spoke.

"Well, all right then. Good luck, Julia. I'm sorry you're going through a lot. You were doing great. Are you sure there's isn't anything you need?"

"No. But thank you. Thank you for watching over me. Your family is very lucky to have you."

"That's very nice of you to say. Again, sorry I was making those phone calls from your room. I'd prefer if you didn't mention it to my supervisor, but I feel bad just telling you what to do. I can't imagine you heard me, but that's no excuse. I'm truly sorry if I disturbed you. Take care okay?"

Much like it was in the night, his voice sounded sweet and soothing—the very best in bedside manner. Julia cursed herself for being so foolish. She smiled politely and nodded a thank you. There was no point in dragging this out. After all, baby girls do look peaceful in their sleep, just as older girls do, when no one is watching.

DREAM LIFE

Jennifer Delozier

Sometimes he wished he could take flight

from the frightful mess that was his life.

In a dream last night,

he had grown wings,

and taken a flying leap off the edge of Mt. Tom, finding himself floating

in the warm updraft along the side of the mountain.

He looked around,

precariously at first, and

saw his dream life began to unfold in the valley below.

He gasped as more of the image came into view.

There was a beautiful tan-colored cottage

with brown trim around the windows and doors.

It was a one-story dwelling with lush green grass in the front and back yards.

The perennial beds filled with tulips, daffodils, and dahlias

hugged the side yards close to the cottage.

As he continued to float downward,

he could see two cats sunning themselves in the front windowsill.

He propelled himself towards the ground until he reached the street.

Stretching his legs, and raising his arms overhead,

he realized his wings were gone.

Had he just reentered the frightful mess that he had tried so hard to leave?

He was stumbling around now, tears in his eyes.

looking for some guidance. Off in the distance, he saw

a white light which seemed to beckon to him.

He felt drawn to it and slowly moved in its direction.

As he entered the light, anxiety and fear dropped away.

The experience was more beautiful than he had imagined.

Could this still be a dream?

It no longer mattered.

On the other side of the light, he

finally found his dream life.

EUGENE

Clare Green

Eugene, my old farmer friend, lived along Rt. 78 in Warwick in his mother's home. He always extended a warm porch welcome to sit a spell as I passed by in the late 1970's. During the days of summer, you could find Eugene porchside. If I happened to drive by in my robin's egg blue VW bug, and have extra time to visit, I'd pull into his driveway and join him in conversation. My two-year-old son and I would enjoy our shared moments with him. His bright blue eyes sparkled while he shared about farm and town lore, and stories from his time of service during World War II. I listened with fascination, bordering on reverence. I imagined the difficulties he must have endured. Now, I thought, here he is. A farmer.

Fondly, I remember him chorusing to me: "The corn is ripe for pickin'—let's go!" and "the blackberries are in. Pick as much as you want. Stop by anytime and get them, even if I'm not here."

And so these small, heartfelt gestures of Yankee kindness touched our hearts as well as our taste buds. As a newly single mom on a limited budget, of course I dearly appreciated the gifts of fresh produce. More than that, I enjoyed sitting on the porch with Eugene and talking. We relaxed. For me, time stood still. It was a small oasis of neighborly thoughtfulness as I learned the ropes of a new town. Eugene helped me to feel at home.

One night, I had a dream. In it, Eugene literally gave me the shirt off his back ... I awoke. Yes, that dream was so true! Eugene would help me in any way he could, and that gesture wasn't out of the ordinary at all.

When fall came, I was able to purchase the winter supply of cordwood we needed from him. He knew I'd need a wheelbarrow, so he just gifted me one of his.

Forty years later, I am still using that gift.

Eugene moved to a nearby hill town when he met the love of his life. Eventually, he married her. A couple of years after that, he and his brother won the lottery. A million bucks. His brother lived in Athol, and Eugene told him to always buy two tickets and that he'd pay his brother back for his ticket when he saw him. It was amazing. They actually won.

There was an Athol Daily News article written about them and their winnings. Eugene was asked, "Now that you have all this money, what are you going to do?" His reply? "I guess I'll go fishin'."

Money wouldn't change Eugene. That was just like him. He and his wife did spend some of it to travel together and explore new sights.

Eugene married late in life and had a wonderful six years. His last bow was a fatal heart attack at the Big E in Springfield. He lives on in my memory as my gentle porchside soul who embraced a young mother and her son.

Every year, when fall arrives and I am faced with the task of stacking wood, one can still find me maneuvering his wheelbarrow and trailing the scent of fresh-cut oak.

In the simplicity of just being, and showing a little old-fashioned neighborly kindness, treasured moments for a lifetime were created.

BOILING POINT

Gina Giorgio

The humidity was oppressive. It was like a living thing—something tangible that could be seen and could envelop the skin in a heavy, clammy embrace. If it had a voice, it would whisper angrily with moist breath in your ear. The August heat wave was unbearable, but being stuck in a traffic gridlock downtown, at noon, in the stifling weather, was literally hell on earth.

Everyone seemed to feel the frustration. In a faded minivan, a young mother sat holding her head in her hands while her children were bickering; she would turn around and yell at them periodically but for the most part she just looked defeated. Meanwhile, a sharp-looking man in a business suit was reclined in the driver's seat of his shiny black BMW, windows up, comfortably closed off from the rest of the world. He was lost in thought, somewhere far away. Pleasantly trapped behind a furniture delivery truck was a top down convertible with two teenage girls in the front and a dreadlocked young man in the back. They moved in unison to the sound of a reggae beat, possibly the only car riding out the traffic jam.

Pedestrians were weaving in and out of the bumper-to-bumper vehicles, more often than not talking on their cell phones or tuned in to some music. They walked, a colorful and uncoordinated parade, sometimes side-by-side, or one-behind-the-other, coming from each side of the street. They were a blend of halter tops and shirts and ties, cut-off denim shorts and flowing sundresses punctuated by too-high sandals, Italian loafers, and running sneakers. Along with those on foot were the ones who rode bikes and zipped by on skateboards. There was even a motorized wheelchair. Whether or not they hurried or swaggered, every single person shared the wilted look of the hot and sweaty.

The buildings loomed large on each side of the clogged passageway, adding to the air of suffocation. Not one leaf on the few trees that lined the sidewalks moved; there was no breeze to stir them. The smell of exhaust fumes nauseated all.

Twenty minutes into the ordeal, the natives were getting restless. Cab drivers began leaning on their horns, with a sing-song chorus of curses as accompaniment. The sharp-looking man in his cool, closed-off world was raking his hands through his hair as he talked on his cell phone with agitation. The young man had tucked his dreadlocks under a cap and was lying down in the back seat of the convertible, eyes closed, while the two girls in the front stared ahead, music low, not talking. One of the children in the minivan had fallen asleep, but the other chattered endlessly to the mother, who had long since given up on any peace and quiet.

By that time, appointments had been missed, lunch breaks were over, and patience had been worn thin.

What was the holdup, here? An accident? Well, sure, that would be too bad but clear it up already! Construction? Figures—the state lets the pot holes go until every vehicle on the road needs a new oil pan and then, when they decide to fill them in, it's in the middle of a day when the weather pattern has traveled straight from Hades. OH, and let's not EVEN get started on the cops directing this mess … What is WRONG with people? What is WRONG with this WORLD? WHY is life SO HARD?

And then a drop appeared on a windshield, and another, then another, until the downpour began. Warm raindrops felt icy in comparison to the air. Leaves stirred in the slight breeze that had started; a young boy on the sidewalk stretched out his arms and did a little dance. He twirled around, loose-limbed, not a care in the world. One of the girls in the convertible tilted her face upwards, closed her eyes, and smiled into the rain. Meanwhile, the motorized top hummed to life in a futile attempt to shelter them from the sudden deluge. Still awake but now silent, the child in the minivan traced the drip of a raindrop on the window, her small finger smearing a semi-permanent trail. The sharp-looking man, still cloistered in his air-conditioned car, turned off his cell phone and turned up the radio. He watched as the world around him moved in some well-choreographed ballet. And then, just like that, the cars began to inch onward with the rest of their lives.

FRESH PAINT
Jennifer Delozier

Bella had decided, long before her husband left, that she needed to give her daughter, Anna, free reign in some areas of Anna's life. This would somehow keep the two of them connected. So, she refrained from barking out orders and doling out restrictions, but wasn't sure how to proceed from there.

The whitewalls of Anna's car had been transformed into a brightly colored green, painted on a warm, dry night between 2 and 4 in the morning while Bella slept. Then, there was the guest bathroom. The sacred walls had been altered from gaudy purple to yellow and orange diagonal stripes. It made Bella almost vomit whenever she stepped through the door. She became dizzy, her eyes glazed over, and she had to hold onto the sink to remain upright.

Anna's hair was a frizzled mess of green and blue, brushed day after day—never wavering or dulling, much to Bella's chagrin. Anna's fingernails were long and curved, black backgrounds with white shots of lightning affixed to each one. She had her nails and hair done every week, bills paid by her mother, of course. Bella spent nights lying awake wondering how she would speak to Anna about her getting a job to pay for her excessive lifestyle. After many sleepless nights, Bella knew it was time to approach her daughter with a no-nonsense attitude. One early summer evening, they sat in the living room. Anna was sucking on the end of a piece of her so-called hairdo while clicking her fingernails on the table next to the overstuffed couch. It was then Bella began to lay out plans for their new life together. Anna would need to get a job that paid significant wages to cover her lurid lifestyle. Then, she would be responsible for renovating and remodeling the farmhouse on their property, tearing down the old roof, and putting up a new one before the beginning of winter. Her work on the farmhouse would continue in the spring. When completed, it was to be Anna's new home, painted however she pleased. Anna was aghast. With a high pitch screech, she bolted from the room.

Satisfied with her newly found motherly control, Bella turned her attention to the rest of the land around their home which overlooked the Pioneer Valley. In addition to the farmhouse, she discovered an ancient storage shed. It was quite dilapidated and overgrown with weeds, most of which climbed and curled up the sides of the shed—disappearing between the outside walls and the peeling gray shingled roof. It seemed to beckon Bella to tackle its renovation. She decided to take the plunge.

One late summer afternoon, Bella was determined to manifest her own version of fresh paint by restoring this ancient storage shed. After the engrossing and daunting work of pulling weeds and removing them from the cracks and crevices, the possibilities of her project's end results became clear. Bella had never engaged in such a humongous task like the one before her. However, Bella determined that on the inside of the shed, the beams and joists were intact. The windows needed cleaning, but the only real job was to strip the old paint off the exterior walls and repaint it before the cool weather of autumn set in. As Bella began, she had thoughts of bathroom walls, with yellow and orange diagonal stripes, and black fingernails with white lightning bolts. She laughed and shook her head. Her version of fresh paint on the shed would be a dull, light brown, but still a secret success. It would replace Anna's decision about her own version of fresh paint.

LAST LAUGH

Diane Kane

When Mr. Munson moved into the decaying farmhouse, he was driving an aging white van with a handicap plate. Each day, I delivered mail to his battered mailbox that hung precariously by a single rusty nail. He didn't have much to say to me, but he called the post office on occasion—looking for his check that had not arrived yet. Whoever had the pleasure of answering his calls got bombarded with a litany of colorful four-letter words, followed by a loud click.

As time went on, the paint on the old farmhouse peeled, and Mr. Munson's van sat permanently with the hood up. Even the trees around the house grew weary and regularly dropped limbs across the driveway.

Years passed, and Mr. Munson's health declined further. When he was not picking up his mail, I became concerned. I made some inquiries and discovered that he was in the Veteran's Hospital. Months later, he called the post office to say in no uncertain terms that he was back.

Mr. Munson had his mailbox moved to his front door. I maneuvered my mail truck around discarded waste and forged a path up his unmaintained walkway in all seasons.

Then, he started to get packages of medication that needed his signature. Spouting obscenities, he opened the door only enough to extend his wrinkled hand. With thick yellow fingernails, he grabbed the slip, scribbled his name, and shoved it back. He grasped the package and slammed the door shut.

I would automatically say, "Have a nice day." Then I would feel bad. How could he ever really have a nice day? I felt sad for the crabby old man who lived alone. I called the local veteran's outreach office. They knew Mr. Munson well.

"We've tried, he won't take any help," the veteran's assistant told me. "You can't force someone to accept aid."

Finally, one day, Mr. Munson couldn't make it to the door, and he let me in. He sat in a wheelchair sparsely dressed in only a ragged white tee shirt. His two amputated legs were clearly visible. From then on, I would knock, and he would shout for me to enter. I always found him lying on his couch with an old western movie blaring on the television. One day he didn't answer, so I opened the door a little wider. I peered over to where Mr. Munson lay sprawled out on his couch with his usual lack of clothing. But this day, his head was tilted back, and lifeless, foggy blue eyes stared back at me. John Wayne walked casually across the television screen, and I screamed.

I stumbled to my truck and called my supervisor, "My customer is dead!"

***

I waited in my mail truck for the authorities and said a prayer for Mr. Munson.

The police officer entered the house and came back out shortly.

"Mr. Munson states that he is very much alive."

"But he looked dead."

"To tell you the truth," the officer said, "he looked dead to me too until he sat up and shouted, 'What the hell are you doing in here?'"

"I guess I have to deliver his package."

"Ahh," the officer hesitated. "Mr. Munson is in a state of undress."

I laughed. "Mr. Munson is always in a state of undress."

Getting up my nerve, I headed for the door and knocked. Mr. Munson's gruff voice shouted for me to enter.

"So, you're the one who reported me dead, huh?"

"Yes, sir."

"Did I scare you?"

"I'm still shaking!"

Mr. Munson let out a bellowing laugh that made me jump.

"Well, I ain't dead yet," he said and pointed to a picture on a shelf amongst the clutter. "I'm pretty tough, you know."

I waded through the debris on the floor to take a closer look at a picture of a proud young man in uniform. I turned to the withering body of that same man and wondered what had gone wrong between then and now. I knew I couldn't fix any of it, but it warmed my heart to see him laughing now, even if it was at my expense.

From then on, each time I brought him a package, Mr. Munson would chuckle and say, "I ain't dead yet."

CLOCKWISE

Diana Lynne Norman

a clock

is wise?

I never knew.

It does make sense though

As it has every opportunity

To muse

and ruminate

On all it sees.

Must be dull,

To do nothing

But hang around

All   the
time.

READ MY FACE

Michael Young

My face is lined and creased leather, like those trappers and traders who came to this valley and the Nipmuc and Abenaki people who greeted them. I came to this valley much later, my family seeking new lands and a fresh opportunity. Only I did not travel the New England rivers or the Long Trail to get here. Instead, I traveled by truck, west to east, with my keeper who migrated from Washington State, via New York and Connecticut. But that is another story.

I languished for years in a cardboard box and lapsed into disuse. My parts no longer worked. I could not even use my hands, which was a great disability, since I had no voice. They were my only means of communication. Yes, I once talked with my hands and with the numbers on my face, but now they had fallen off. My new lease on life came when my keeper freed me from the box, gave me a new motor and hands, and fastened new numerals onto my face. You see, I'm a clock!

My keeper was not my maker. That was Uncle Don, who lived on the Washington Coast. He had been an Air Force veteran from the Korean War era who joined the military after a colorful adolescence. Everyone recognized his souped-up Mercury driving around town with its long, police-style whip antenna out the back. He was known to the police whom he imitated. Perhaps he was urged by the court to join the military to settle him down. He looked rather dashing in his Air Force uniform with its silver buttons and his hat at a jaunty angle. His future looked bright.

But the only thing Uncle Don got out of the service was a crippling paralysis of unknown origin—paralyzing his muscles which wantedto walk and breathe. He landed in a military hospital outside Seattle, which would save his life, yet from which the doctors said he would never leave. At first, he was confined to an iron lung like victims of polio. Then, he was assisted in his breathing by a plastic bubble, strapped to his chest. Gradually, through rehab and medication, Uncle Don was able to move around in a wheelchair during the day. Not as racy as his V8 Merc, but at least his wheels set him free. He only needed his assisted breathing bubble during the night.

His exuberant spirit in the face of adversity, or maybe his red hair and unstoppable good humor, got the attention of his attending nurse, Nan. Her heart went out to him, not in pity, but in admiration. His wild spirit did not deserve to be confined to the dull, drab halls of a medical institution. Nan was determined to get him out of there. First, they got married. Love turned to devotion, lover to caregiver.

With the proper medications and equipment, Uncle Don was able to leave the hospital. He and Nan settled on Whidbey Island in Puget Sound. Their mobile home perched between woods as well as fields of berries which could be cultivated for wine. While it was not as wild as his youth, his life was wild enough. His experience with cars gave him a way to enhance his mobility. Even before the invention of handicap vans, Uncle Don bought a used bread truck and fitted it out as a camper, complete with a portable generator. He could travel in it, sleep in it, and have his portable breathing equipment in it, which he now used only when sleeping. Uncle Don and Nan hit the road. They drove the Alcan Highway through British Columbia, but not all the way to Alaska. Finally, he was free.

When he was not on an adventure with Nan, Uncle Don was crafting leather works. While his legs may not have functioned, his hands did in a fashion. Through practice, he learned to tool leather, which is how I came to be. As a Christmas present, I was created by my maker with a leather face and a wooden frame. The flowing lines of my floral design were set off by metal numerals. A battery-powered motor drove my hands so I could tell the time. They pointed to a timeless message, which my keeper says to this day, "If Uncle Don could do it, so can you!"

Better get to work. It's time.

IN THE END

Steven Michaels

We know Ozymandias got it wrong

yet we still cannot espouse the lesson.

When the saints of Abbey Road tried

to summarize it by equation

they solidified their own.

Were it ever so simple.

The real danger is not in what we do

But what our followers do.

How can Jesus have a second coming

when His invite has gone to hell?

History is writ by winning streaks,

only those who've had the most to lose

get mentioned in the wake.

Who decides our legacy?

The admin of the world or Mother Earth?

We have to make our own.

But nothing lasts forever

unless you imprint it on the soul.

Beating hearts of black or red

Will carry that weight a long time.

Be wary then of the change you make

and balance the equation of Love and Take.

THE SIDEWALK ON VALLEY ROAD

James Thibeault

Daniel struggled to roll up the hill—his wheels dodging cracks and pivots in the concrete. Cars whizzed by as his wheelchair progressed like a tortoise. Meanwhile, all of the hares would be home, resting on their couches, watching reality TV, long before Daniel finished the race. It often took him twenty minutes or more to reach the top—a thirty second drive or a five minute walk. However, to get home, he had to muscle his way up Valley Rd every single day. It was unavoidable, but Daniel never complained. He just grunted and pushed his metal seat inch by inch.

He tried to think positively: at least it wasn't winter. They never salted the sidewalks on this road and the drainage above sometimes coated the concrete in black ice. Those days Daniel took his chance on the road, but the barrage of honking discouraged him from doing it often. There was also the time that he was clipped by a car—which drove off while Daniel was knocked off his seat. The car never stopped, knowing full-well the lawsuit Daniel would bring down on him. Therefore, it was mostly the sidewalks for Daniel nowadays, except when there was none. Many of the roads only had breakdown lanes for him, and it always gave him anxiety. He could avoid Valley Rd altogether, take some side roads that would only add another fifteen to his commute. However, many of those side streets lacked sidewalks and that hit-and-run deterred him from taking those chances.

Grunting and gripping the wheels with his gloved hands— Daniel lost his concentration as a motorized chair drove up beside him.

"What's up Dan, how's the hill?" The electric seat slowed down to Daniel's painful pace.

"Curt, not now. If I stop, it's hard to start again. You know this."

"Oh come on. It ain't that bad. Your biceps could crush walnuts right now."

"These biceps want to crush your head."

Curt cocked back his head and laughed. He had a bright white smile and was quite chipper despite his recent paralysis. Was it six months, seven? Daniel didn't remember, but he would never forget dealing with Curt's constantly whining during rehabilitation. Dan worked with those transitioning to wheelchairs as a counselor. Dan never knew the loss of movement, as he was born disabled, but for people like Curt—losing the ability to walk was like losing a part of themselves. Curt refused to talk to anybody for a while, and he was often found brooding by the window. Anger, frustration, depression—these emotions cycled through Curt as Daniel worked with him. Eventually, Daniel got through to him, and Curt learned to adjust to his new circumstances—not accept it—but move away from the endless sulking with no solution.

"Come on Dan-the-man," said Curt mockingly, "I'm just trying to keep you company. Do you have to be so negative?"

"Will you just go?"

"Nah, this is more fun. Did you fill out that application yet?"

Daniel groaned. It didn't matter how many times Daniel refused, Curt always insisted he apply for the motorized chair. A foundation recently donated several motorized wheelchairs for citizens in desperate need. While Daniel had limited use of his legs, he could technically traverse the city with little assistance. Those motorized chairs were for people who were significantly impaired. That didn't stop Curt from applying.

"This baby can hit eleven miles per hour. Watch me fly up this hill."

While it wasn't exactly flying, Curt sped past Daniel—who was beginning to breathe heavily.

"I'm … fine … just go."

"Please," Curt stopped and waited for Daniel to catch up. "You don't have to lie. On the application, one of the questions is 'Do you struggle on your daily commute'. Are you struggling?"

"It's … part of life."

"Dude, you were born into this shit. I wasn't. You never knew what it's like to jump, to sprint. Now, I have to sit on my ass all day?"

"Lucky you … tell me more about this 'walking'. What's it like?"

"I'm sorry, that was uncalled for."

"Just go."

"Look, there can't be that many people that 100 percent qualify. You have a chance to make your life easier, and you're turning it down."

"Leave!" Daniel stopped, gripped the wheel, and spoke to the ground—face completely red. "A T3 injury! Constantly complaining about never walking again. Jesus, after that damage, it's a miracle to even have use of hands. Couldn't even use them for four weeks. At first, he was barely breathing on his own—hooked up on tubes. Oh, I used to see him in rehab, his aide parking him in a corner—ditching him while she chatted with the other assistants. I would try to talk to him, but all his words were muffed and incoherent as he stared out the window. But I would stay with him—telling him to not give up, but he continued to stare out the window. I pointed out how he could still use his thumb and be thankful for that. Then, one day, he comes in thumbing a joy-stick—with a giant smile on his face. Finally, he was able to control a fraction of his life."

Curt stared at his thumb, then tucked it under his hand.

"I get your point, no need to be so passive."

"Fine. In a few weeks, *you* gained control of the rest of your fingers, then *your* whole arms. Like that! With confidence, all the rehabilitation increased two-fold. Imagine if there wasn't an extra motorized chair for you? If I knew I took that opportunity away from someone, I would fly down Valley Rd into oncoming traffic. So don't you tell me that I'm struggling. I'm fine."

Curt paused, tried to say one thing, then instead rolled his eyes.

"Whatever, keep doing the right thing, I'm sure everyone will admire you for it."

His battery jumped back to life and soon Curt was over the hill and gone. Daniel took a few deep breaths, gripped the wheels, and resumed the climb.

THE JOINING
David M. Barry

On the day I turned eighteen, as the sun rose over the valley, I hiked all the way to Suicide Gorge—feeling as light as the empty backpack resting on my shoulders. I was so ready for this.

When I reached the top, I saw that Wendy was already waiting for me. She stood right in the middle of the path that led to the edge.

She said, "You don't need to do this, Annabelle. I love you the way you are."

"I love you too baby, but, right now, you need to move. Meet me down at the bottom. And don't even think of pulling me out of the pool."

I filled my backpack with a large assortment of rocks. I stripped down to my sports bra and spandex bottoms, squatted low, and looped my arms back through the shoulder straps of my weighted backpack. By the time I lurched to a standing position and steadied myself, I saw that Wendy had moved. I knew she would. She usually did what I asked. Funny, I was a tiny thing—nothing special. She was this Amazon princess. But, I called the shots in our relationship.

"Please, Annabelle," she said, "It's too risky."

I said, "No risk, no reward."

Then, I breathed in deeply and sprinted down the dirt path. I leapt off the highest jagged ledge, plummeting through the air—legs kicking, arms waving. I landed in The Joining Pool and plunged straight to the bottom of the basin. There I gulped in frigid water, felt the stabbing pain, the rush of panic. As the concentration of carbon dioxide in my blood grew toxic, I reminded myself that something extraordinary was about to happen, something that would fix me, or at least make me normal.

It was a shame that I had to die. But that's how The Joining worked. There was something in the water of The Joining Pool. Adults had their theories—don't they always?—but no one really knew what it was. We did know that when The Something in the water entered your lungs, The Something entered your blood. Once it was in your blood, it entered your brain. Then you died. Then The Something found the reboot button in your brain, bringing you back to life. That's when it joined with your consciousness. It created a new and improved version of you—most of the time.

I told myself it was no big deal. Teens in my town did it all the time—had for generations. I used to think it was some kind of trick adults played on us: like Santa Claus and religion. Then I started seeing the results in my own friend group. One after one, I watched them turn eighteen, consent to the Joining, and somehow emerge from The Joining Pool as well-adjusted adults. Friends, who were clueless about what they wanted in life, suddenly had found their calling, their bliss, their tribe. Off they went to live a fulfilling life, all happy and shit. I wanted that! Were there risks? Sure. Apparently, there was a chance that The Something would bury you deep in your own subconscious, take control over your mind and body. People called it The Hostile Takeover. Whatever, I thought, better to be buried inside myself than feel what I was feeling. Like I said to Wendy: no risk, no reward.

Dying sucked. The pain started in my temples. It throbbed, then it stabbed—like knitting needles being pushed into my skull. I tried to scream, but the fluid in my lungs muted me. My efforts caused the muscles in my chest to twist and tighten like they had been caught in a medieval torture device. The last thought on my mind before my brain succumbed to the oxygen deprivation was: *I hope rebirth is easier.*

It wasn't. Rebirth burned like hell, as if my brain were being ignited by a bed of coals. If I wasn't submerged in ice cold water, I swear my skull would have burst into flames. I don't know how long the blaze lasted—seemed like hours. Eventually, the embers in my mind cooled, and I regained control of my body. I removed the backpack from my shoulders and floated to the surface. Once there, I crawled out of the pool like some Darwinian creature emerging from the primordial sea. Then I vomited all The Joining fluid from my lungs and began to breathe normal air.

Soon, I started to feel a warm glow inside my chest. It grew stronger by the second. I thought about how Wendy liked to talk about feeling comfortable in your own skin, how important that was. I would always say to her, "If I had skin like yours I'd feel comfortable all the time." She usually laughed. Truth was, she knew how much I yearned to feel that comfort she had, that wholeness—instead of the fragmented mess of my mind and body. For a moment, after emerging from the pool, I started to feel what I thought Wendy must have felt. Colors popped like I had never seen before. Sounds moved over me like a caress. I smelled the aromas and tasted the sweet air. My skin, the bumpy blemished thing that once trapped me inside my body, now felt the wind and the thousand textures of the ground at my feet. Was this what Wendy experienced? Was this how people felt life? It was all so amazing. But then The Something turned my senses against me.

It created the taste of rancid meat in my mouth, the smell of decay in my nose, the sound of metal scrapping porcelain in my ears. It painted my world blood red and puke green. Everything I touched stabbed my skin. A light rain fell, and the water droplets pelted my body like a thousand needles.

This was how The Hostile Takeover started.

By the time Wendy came down from the cliff, I was laying by the water's edge, whimpering. I pulled myself together as Wendy lifted me up. She knew immediately that the worst-case scenario happened.

"How much time do we have?" She asked, reaching out to cup my face in her hands.

I winced at her touch. "Not long."

"We need to take you to Dr. B., right now."

"Too late."

"She can put you under hypnosis, tame The Something. Maybe even get rid of it."

"You know that's not how it works."

Once The Hostile Takeover began, the only person who could fight it off was you. Wendy knew that. My therapist, Dr. B, had been trying to teach me the skills to tame The Something for years, but I could never get the hang of it. Wendy knew that too. Soon, The Something would bury me deep in the grey matter of my own brain. There was no stopping it.

"Dammit, Annabelle. Why did you have to do this? What am I supposed to do now, sit and watch you suffer?"

I didn't answer her right away. I couldn't tell her what I was thinking. Most people didn't hit the genetic lottery like she did. Her privilege made her blind. She couldn't possibly have known the impact my drug-addicted mother and schizophrenic father had on my development. The Joining had been my best chance for a normal life— or so I thought.

What would have been the point of saying those things? All I really wanted to do was have one last decent moment with her. "You could give me one of those awesome temple massages of yours."

She perked up a little at this. "Do you really think it will help?"

I knew she would feel better if she thought it would help, so I said, "If you do it gently enough."

Wendy placed the tips of her long, delicate fingers onto the soft indentations on both sides of my head. She moved them in slow, circular motions.

Eventually, she asked, "Does that make it any better, sweetie?"

I knew The Something would soon find its way to the language center of my brain, and once there, it would take my words away from me. I figured I would make the most of the words I had left, even if the words I spoke to Wendy were a lie.

I said to her, "Yes, baby. You're making me feel so much better."

WHY

Bryan T. Foley

Over the years I have been asked why I stayed in the military for so long. My response is similar to that of my brothers and sisters who say it's for each other—doing what we do for the man or woman next to us, shoulder to shoulder, covering and being covered by the Marine, Soldier, Airman, Seaman, and Coast Guard. They might also say they joined for a specific reason: money for college. In truth, we weren't going to college, but a choice between service or jail (yes, there are some). For others, it was a personal pride in service to our country, or to learn a skill or trade that would be of some use after the military.

Others have asked, "Don't you think it's time for someone else?" The answer is a little more difficult to explain. The short answer would be, "Yeah, let someone else go." But that's not really the way I feel. In 2008, when I and five other members of the 110th Maintenance Company volunteered to go, I was married and had three children in ages ranging from 6 to 14. My thoughts then were I'm already enlisted, already trained, already a leader as a Sergeant, and all ready to go. If I wanted to volunteer, then maybe another soldier would not get "voluntold". My choosing to go and serve ensured the free will of another soldier who didn't need to be ordered back into action.

I remember back to 2002. It was August or September, just a few months prior to being deployed. At the time, my unit, the 180th Engineer Detachment, trained at Camp Edwards on Cape Cod. During drill weekends, if I didn't have to stay on base at night, I would stay at my mom's a few miles outside the South gate. On this day, we had a few extra hours for chow, and I was invited to join my mom and my stepdad for lunch at a local restaurant on the water in Falmouth. I had on my BDU's (Army camouflage uniform, called at the time, Battle

Dress Uniform). I arrived a few minutes after my parents and was taken to the table by the waitress. I sat down, ordered a soda (yes, I wanted a beer, but I was on duty, and I take that duty seriously). After a few minutes of small talk, a woman, maybe in her early 60's, came over to our table and stood next to me. I didn't know her, but I looked up at her and smiled. She asked me if I was being deployed. I said "Yes." She put her hand on my shoulder and said, "Thank you". Then she bent down closer to me and put her arm around my shoulder, then said in a whisper, "Please be safe and God Bless." Before leaving, she gave me a gentle squeeze and kissed me on the forehead like a mother saying good night to her child.

I never saw this woman again except for those times I have revisited the memory. That's why I served, not for that woman particularly, but for the people of America. It's for those special moments where someone I didn't know took time to wish me safe. At the time, and even now, the emotion of overwhelming pride comes back to me. For we are all God's children meant to care for one another.

THE RUBBLE MOUNTAINS OF BERLIN

Dennis King

I was stationed in the U.S. Army in Berlin—the center of Europe for centuries. Hitler and the Nazis called it home, and the future capital of the world. Their vision was that all the Strasses, Alleys, and Wegs would lead into Berlin. The young architect, Albert Speer, put these grandeur plans on paper. Then, the Allies united and stood up to the Nazis in battle. The Nazis were hunted down and killed, and the capital was bombed for months—killing anyone in range. That is what happens to the enemy in war.

Twenty five years later, I stood on top of a mountain in Berlin—looking out at the city's outskirts. It is a flat terrain except for these two mountains. One was the flat top area reserved for military and civilian satellite equipment called Devil's Mountain—which was off limits to the public. The other one was designated as a people's mountain, with plenty of grassy fields, paved paths, soccer fields, and a beautiful view. The Berliners liked their Sunday outings with picnics as their families peacefully enjoyed the day—feeling a little closer to the heavens.

The irony of all this scenery, family outings, and lofty heights was that these two mountains were man-made, like the stone-by-stone pyramids of antiquity. Germans were forced to endure back-breaking work every day, all day, with very little food or comfort. They did not matter, no one cared about them—they just had to get the work done. These rubble mountains, or *schuttberg,* were built from the destroyed buildings, homes, roads, and debris collected from the bombed-out city of Berlin. The surviving Germans were put to work—mostly women and children—to clean up the destruction of their city.

Wagon by wagon, they shoveled debris from their destroyed country. These now peaceful mountains were the results of Hitler, Nazism, and the nation's choice to kill—starting with the Jewish people.

THE FOUNDER OF QUABBIN QUILLS

Steven Michaels is the author of *Sweet Life of Mystery*, a parody of the whodunit genre. He has been featured on The Satirist website for his scintillating take on current affairs, and has written and produced over twenty plays for students through his work as an afterschool drama coach. Steve founded the Quabbin Quills in 2017 and was instrumental in creating the first anthology, *Time's Reservoir.* He is so thankful to all the authors who have come to share his writer's dream.

ABOUT OUR PUBLISHER

Garrett Zecker is the publisher and co-founder of Quabbin Quills. He holds an MA in English from Fitchburg State University and an MFA in Fiction from Southern New HampshireUniversity's Mountainview MFA. He founded Perpetual Imagination in 2004, specializing in independent releases and live events. Garrett is a writer, actor, and teacher of writing and literature. Links to his work, including other publications, full Shakespeare In The Park performances, and hundreds of book and movie reviews can be found at his blog, GarrettZecker.com.

ABOUT OUR EDITORIAL BOARD MEMBERS

Ruth DeAmicis has worked as a journalist for more than 30 years. Her desire to write fiction has been a dream and a hobby, piling up in notebooks and scraps forever. Now is the time to shake the dust off and get it out there. Her writing about New England just comes naturally.

David Barry is a psychotherapist who writes genre fiction. He hails from Worcester, Massachusetts, where he spends his leisure time with his life partner, her daughter, their dog Lola, and a cat named Mouse. You can follow David (and Lola) on Twitter at @DavidMBarry.

Clare Green is an author and educator, from Warwick and has been clairvoyant since childhood. She offers her insights silently or verbally when asked. Clare welcomes folks to enjoy a cup of tea while visiting her fairy cottage or walk the woodland labyrinth for peace and reflection.

Charlotte Taylor has published short stories and poetry as well as hoards a collection of unedited novels. She loves the process of creating characters, stories, and worlds. Charlotte is an active blogger for her work in Ayurveda and yoga. She is actively seeking a life of peace, study, and fun. Charlotte can often be found surrounded by cats with a mug of tea and reading books. Other times, you'll find her practicing yoga, climbing mountains, and sometimes crawling under barbed wire.

Karen Lynne Traub is a professional belly dancer with a passion for the public library. A student in the inaugural 2020 class of the Newport MFA, her first publishing success was an essay about her failed critical thesis http://bit.ly/goodridd. She is an empty nester living in the woods of the Swift River Valley of western Massachusetts with her husband Frank and her royal python Chloe. Karen is writing a memoir about surviving the war over a new library in her small town of Shutesbury.

James Thibeault is the Treasurer and an executive board member of Quabbin Quills. He is also the author of two young adult novels, *Deacon's Folly* and *Michael's Black Dress*. You can find both books on Amazon or Barnes & Noble as well as follow him @thibeaultauthor on Twitter or JamesThibeaultAuthor on Instagram.

Sonya Wirtanen lives in Phillipston, Massachusetts and has loved writing ever since she learned to rhyme. It was not until recently that she began taking her passion more seriously. Her inspiration comes from her experience as an educator, a foster parent, a yoga teacher, and most recently as an AmeriCorps volunteer. She is also the Secretary and an executive board member for Quabbin Quills. Sonya finds that writing teaches her to live more mindfully by reflecting on the places she has been and the people she meets—taking time to slow down and enjoy the present moment.

Michael Young lives and writes in Royalston, MA on Greenfyre Farm with his wife, two mini horses, and a large dog. He has had pieces published in *A Time for Singing*, *A Certain Slant*, and *The Princeton Wineskin*, along with magazine inclusions in *Trout* and *Grit*. This is his second appearance in a Quabbin Quills anthology. His love of nature, coupled with his passion for fishing, often colors his writing.

ABOUT OUR SCHOLARSHIP RECIPIENTS

Quabbin Quills was established in 2017 by a group of writers banded together by the common love of writing. In addition to publishing anthologies, we also wanted to foster creativity, highlight young talent, and give back to our community. Our High School Scholarship is a cash prize given to the top three young writers from the Quabbin area who have participated in our free workshops and present an enthusiastic and energetic spirit in approaching the writing prompt for the anthology. We are proud to include this year's recipients in Voices of the Valley and provide funds that they can use however they like in pursuit of their writing and postsecondary education: Cecelia Januszewski, Aidan Needle, and Matthew Shepardson.

All nonprofit proceeds from Quabbin Quills' publications are reinvested in educational programs, publications and operations, and yearly scholarships for young writers.

Cecilia Januszewski is eighteen years old and lives in Oakham with her family and her wonderful dog. She enjoys art in all its forms, and in addition to writing, loves acting and dancing. Though she has always loved the written word, this is her first published work. She is grateful to Quabbin Quills for publishing her story and hopes to continue writing in the future.

Aidan Needle is a junior at Athol High School. This is his first publication of poetry and is grateful for every opportunity Quabbin Quills has given him. Aidan aspires to study screenwriting at NYU or UCLA and eventually become a filmmaker. He would like to thank his family for buying him his first journal, which houses his poems outside of future literary magazines. He is grateful for the Brandeis summer program (Bima) which inspired these works, as well as his friends for being the best source of laughs and love. He especially wishes to thank Grant for reading his work and pushing him to write his very best.

Matthew Shepardson is a young author and outdoor enthusiast. Never much into writing or math, he surprised himself one day with an idea to write a poem, and it came out great. He did the lighting and backstage work for the drama club in middle school and worked on the prom committee in high school. Although he does not consider himself the most popular kid in school, Quabbin Quills is most pleased with his talent!

ABOUT OUR CONTRIBUTORS

Jon Bishop is a Massachusetts-based writer and poet. He is co-editor and co-founder of *Portrait of New England* and co-founder of *The JT Lit Review*, a literary blog. His work has appeared in *The Arts Fuse*, *Burning House Press*, *Mountains and Meditations*, *Fourth & Sycamore*, *Laurel Magazine*, *Boston Literary Magazine*, and *Liberty Island*, among other publications. His first book of poetry, *Scratching Lottery Tickets on a Street Corner*, was published in 2018 by Finishing Line Press.

Kathleen Bennett, a turn of the century poet and writer, has published her poetry in local and international anthologies as well as several articles in area newspapers. Her first book was released in 2019. Her piece was inspired by the spectacular view of Tully Lake and Mountain, and it felt fitting to share in *Voices of the Valley.* Whatever is lovely, whatever is pure, right, and true inspires her. Kathleen now shares her spiritual inspiration of hope and faith on her website: bountynow.net.

Kathy Chencharik lives across the road from the Millers River in the North Quabbin area, where she likes to capture wildlife in the lens of her camera. She is a free-lance writer whose poetry, non-fiction, and fiction have appeared in several newspapers, magazines, and anthologies. She won the *Derringer Award* for best flash fiction for *"The Book Signing"* in *Thin Ice (a Level Best Books anthology, 2010).* She earned numerous honorable mentions in *Alfred Hitchcock Mystery Magazine's "The Story That Won"* contest; eight of which are included in *Flash in the Can.*

Phyllis Cochran retired early from a career in business and became a freelance inspirational writer. Her work has appeared in *Chicken Soup for the Soul* books, *Woman's World, Grit, Focus on the Family,* and various magazines as well as several anthologies. She has taught Writing for Publication and Memoir classes. Her book *Shades of Light—A Spiritual Memoir* was published in 2006. Phyllis enjoys caring for her grandchildren and family dogs when needed.

Kay Deans lives on a small farm in north central Massachusetts with her husband Peter, her German shepherd dog Lady, and an eclectic collection of goats, sheep, and guardian animals. Also, an occasional pig and pony. She was the founding editor of *CryoGas International* and has more than 40 feature articles published in *New England Country Folks* and *Country Folks Grower.*

Jennifer Delozier has been writing since she was 10 years old. She started with a diary, locked of course, which her brother broke into and read her most private thoughts and feelings. She enjoyed having a feature in her high school's literary magazine. Having moved to the Pioneer Valley 26 years ago, she has since submitted four Letters to the Editor and one Guest Column that were accepted by the Gazette. Jennifer now lives in Easthampton. At age 64, her continuous diaries and poetry inspire her to continue writing.

Bryan T. Foley was born and raised in between Massachusetts and Maine, graduating from Skowhegan Area High School, class of 86. Bryan then enlisted in the United States Marine Corps and later attended the Massachusetts Maritime Academy. In 2001, prior to 9-11, Bryan enlisted in the Massachusetts Army National Guard and was deployed twice to Kuwait and Iraq. He completed his service obligation in 2017. Bryan didn't begin writing until 2017, after inpatient treatment at the North Hampton VA facility. Bryan lives with his wife Eileen and their three boys in Winchendon, along with two German Shepherds, three cats, and two fish.

Gina Giorgio is a librarian and freelance writer from Rhode Island. A married mother of two and stepmom of two, she also shares a home with a bunch of cute but crazy fur babies. She is an avid reader, a music enthusiast, vegetarian, and an animal lover. Find Gina on Twitter @gnagiso, Instagram @gigio122, LinkedIn, and Facebook.

Sharon A. Harmon is a freelance writer and poet. She writes for the *Uniquely Quabbin Magazine*. She has two chapbooks of poetry *Swimming with Cats* and *Wishbone in a Lightning Jar* (Flutter Press, 2017). She has been published in *Silkworm, Green living, Compass Roads, Worcester Magazine* and numerous other publications. She has stories in *Chicken Soup for the Soul, Birds & Blooms,* and flash fiction in *Flash in the Can One* and *Flash in the Can Two*. She has taught writers workshops and is currently working on two children's books. She also does book marketing consultations. She lives deep in the woods of Royalston. Find her at Sharon A. Harmon Writer & Poet on Facebook.

Diane Kane is a published author of fiction and non-fiction stories. She writes articles for the *Uniquely Quabbin Magazine* and is one of the original founding members of Quabbin Quills. Diane loves to help other authors achieve their goals. She does proofreading, book formatting, and publishing. Follow her on Facebook at Page of Possibilities and online at www.WriteofPossibilities.com. Diane lives in a small rural town in Western Massachusetts and spends her summers on the rocky shores of Maine chasing her dreams of writing.

Eileen P. Kennedy lives in Amherst, MA with the ghost of Emily Dickinson. They migrate together in cold weather to Costa Rica. Her chapbook *Banshees* (Flutter Press, 2015) was nominated for a Pushcart Prize in 2015 and awarded Second Prize from the Wordwrite Book Awards in Poetry. She was awarded Second Prize in the Penumbra Haiku Poetry Contest. She was a finalist for the 2018 Concrete Wolf Louis Poetry Prize. She won Honorable Mention from the New England, New York and London Book Festivals, as well as from the Tom Howard/Margaret Reid/Poetry Contest and the Oregon Poetry Society. More at EileenPKennedy.com.

Diana Lynne Norman, a transplant from rural Pennsylvania, now lives in Western Massachusetts with her husband, two homeschooled children, and their cat. Diana has created numerous stories to share in the oral tradition at library story times and has had many poems and short stories, both fiction and non-fiction, printed in various publications.

Sally Sennott is a graduate of Duke University. She was a longtime resident of Athol and recently moved to Belmont, MA. As a retired newspaper correspondent and editor of a local museum newsletter, she honed her writing skills. Sally has authored two plays as well as a children's story that were produced into videos and featured on the Athol cable access channel AOTV. A contributor to the anthologies *Time's Reservoir* and *Mountains and Meditations,* she aspires to write fiction for the New Yorker.

Christina Sutcliffe is a local English Professor, writer, hiker, gardener, and mother. She loves to look at the natural world, at the varieties of life, and learn. She writes for the same reason she teaches: to open eyes and minds.

Jan VanVaerenewyck has been creating since before she could write. Her poetry, essays, and quilts appear in various publications. She is a member of the Louise Bogan Chapter of the Massachusetts State Poetry Society.

Made in the USA
Middletown, DE
24 July 2020